Dirty Money Honey

Dirty Money Honey

Erica Hilton
Nisa Santiago
and Introducing
Kim K.

Dirty Money Honey. Copyright © 2011 by Melodrama Publishing. All rights reserved. Printed in the United States of America. No part of this book may be used or reproduced in any manner whatsoever without written permission except in the case of brief quotations embodied in critical articles or reviews. For information, address Melodrama Publishing, P.O. Box 522, Bellport, NY 11713.

www.melodramapublishing.com

Library of Congress Control Number: 2011927243
ISBN-13: 978-1934157442
ISBN-10: 1934157449
First Edition: September 2011
10 9 8 7 6 5 4 3 2 1

Interior Design: Candace K. Cottrell
Cover Design: Marion Designs
Cover Model: Renata

The Mastermind

♠ Nisa Santiago ♠

mas·ter·mind (mstr-mnd)
n.

*A highly intelligent person, especially
one who plans and directs a complex or difficult
project: the mastermind of a robbery.*

*tr.v. mas·ter·mind·ed, mas·ter·mind·ing, mas·ter·minds
To direct, plan, or supervise (a project or activity).*

Intro

East Harlem, NY

2009

It was a bitterly cold day in December and there I was, Honey Robertson, sitting in on my first raid with my immediate supervisor, James Dougherty, a hard-drinking, tough-talking Irish-American. I'd been working as an agent for the Bureau of Alcohol, Tobacco, Firearms and Explosives, better known as the ATF, for six short months. My health insurance had kicked in, my checks were being direct-deposited into my checking account, and I'd even signed up for their 401(k) plan, where I was investing heavily into different stocks and United States Treasury bonds. Not bad for a 23-year-old female from Harlem.

"How much longer do you think we'll have to wait?"

"How the fuck should I know some stupid shit like that?" James quipped. "And why you asking anyways? You're getting paid for each second you sit here doing nothing. Like, what the fuck are you doing right now that I gotta hear you complaining?"

Not many females would be able to take his direct talk, but I felt he was a breath of fresh air. Sure, he was abrasive, but I wasn't a sensitive type of chick. In fact, if he was all polite talk and stuffy, it would have taken me longer to open up and trust him.

"I got a stiff black penis that needs the attention of my mouth tonight."

James laughed. "And that takes precedence over possibly apprehending a terrorist? A small black penis?"

"Who said *small*, muthafucka?"

"Ain't all black penises small?" James arched his eyebrow and smirked. He definitely found himself amusing.

I looked at his puffy face, a telltale sign of years of alcohol abuse. It was a look I knew too well. His skin, which should have been pale white, was tinged with a fuchsia pink. Though slightly overweight, he was a handsome man, but he always looked flustered and overworked, and had that "cop air" a seasoned criminal could spot a mile away.

I took another sip of my now warm coffee and thought about Dré, who I'd married two days after my eighteenth birthday and was still head over heels in love with. We'd grown up in the same building in Lexington housing projects in East Harlem, New York. He'd sold drugs hand-to-hand, but within a few years he began pushing weight and even had a few soldiers under his belt.

My brother Chief had fucked up Dré's work, and Dré came around to collect. He'd shot up Chief in the hallway of our building, and Chief had crawled to our front door with Dré looming over him. Chief took two bullets, one in the abdomen, and one just grazed his temple. I'd heard the shots and came running out the front door and stood face-to-face with Dré holding a .357 to Chief's head at point-blank range. I pleaded with him not to finish him off, and for some inexplicable reason, he lowered his pistol and slowly backpedaled, never taking his eyes off me.

Before that unfortunate incident, Dré, fourteen years my senior, didn't look twice at me, who, at the time, was a 16-year-old school nerd, focused on getting out of the PJs.

"So much for counterintelligence," James said haphazardly. "I think we're in for a long night. This muthafucka might have us out here breaking day, which is good. I need the overtime."

I exhaled. As much as I loved my job and was grateful that the Federal Bureau had hired me, I loved spending my nights with Dré. Sitting in an undercover car waiting only God knows how many hours on a possible terrorist wasn't appealing.

I pulled out my cell phone and dialed Dré. "Hey, babe," I said. "It looks like we're gonna pull an overnighter."

"What about dinner?" he asked.

"Umm, there's some spaghetti in there from last night, and the salad." I thought quickly. "Or you could make yourself a hamburger."

"Yo, you gotta do something about this job of yours!"

"Do something?"

"You know what the fuck I mean. They can't have you out at all types of night when you got a household to hold down."

"It ain't like this happens all—"

"Don't give me that bullshit. I don't give a fuck about all that you talkin'. You got me up in here cookin' and cleanin' up shit. What the fuck I need you for?"

"I'm not your maid, Dré."

"You're my wife!"

"Exactly!" I wanted to say more, but who wants to air their marital laundry out in front of their boss?

"A'ight, I don't got time for this bickering shit. I'll see you in the morning."

I could sense he wanted to continue the argument but chose not to.

Dré had a warped vision of women and my duties as his wife. When I told him I was applying to be an ATF agent, he thought he'd hit the jackpot of wives. He thought that meant he'd have a get-out-of-jail-free card, which I later explained wasn't the case. For some odd reason he felt that I would contact local and state police and also all federal agents and announce to them that my husband Dré Robertson could move as much drugs as he pleased and to not fuck with him, or else. Once I drilled into his head how asinine his rationale was, it was back to him thinking a woman's place was in the bedroom and kitchen.

So, although I was a young wife, I handled mines. I kept a clean house, fucked Dré whenever he wanted to be fucked and, except on nights like these, kept his meals on the table.

"You don't look too happy?"

"I'm good."

"He hates your long hours?"

"Something like that."

"Fuck 'im."

"Is that your advice? 'Cuz if so, I'll pass." I rolled my eyes playfully. "Besides, you have three ex-wives. You're hardly in the position to be dishing out advice, with your track record."

"Two. I have two ex-wives," Dougherty corrected.

"Whatever."

I reclined my seat, slightly, and propped my feet up on the dashboard. I needed to think about my marriage and how Dré spoke to me. After tonight I intended on things changing. Dré was the only person who I allowed to fully rule over me, and I did it because I was his wife. He treated me like some side chick.

Dougherty tapped the side of my leg. "Move your feet." He then reached into his glove compartment and pulled out a flask of whiskey. "Might as well lighten the mood."

"We're on the clock."

"So?"

"So any minute we're about to do a full-on raid on an armed, dangerous fugitive for selling weapons—AK-47s, Uzis, Glocks, the whole gamut. We can't be fucked up."

"Honey, I'm Irish. A pint of whiskey can't get my four-year-old daughter fucked up."

"But what about backup, car 44-10? What if they smell it on us?"

"Jesus, Honey! I'm not even drunk and you're blowing my high. I'm your supervisor, and you're my subordinate. Let me worry about the other car. If one of them even opened up their mouths to say something foul, I'll fucking punch their teeth down their throats! All the shit I've seen go down out here while we're on a stakeout is shit you'd have to see to believe. One thing you gotta learn is that we have a brotherhood. Whatever is done out in the field stays there. You got me?"

I shook my head. "Well, you know I'm down for whatever."

"Then shut the fuck up"—James flashed a broad smile—"and drink."

An hour into our hardcore drinking, I was giggling and cracking jokes, yet neither one of us was drunk, despite the fact that we'd down the whiskey and had now mixed it with a liter of Scotch Dougherty found in his back seat. Honestly, I wasn't a whiskey or Scotch type of girl. I was more Moët or margaritas, but the randomness of the night made it fun.

"So how much does a pair of fancy sneakers like you got on cost ya?"

"These?" I replied, looking down at my Prada kicks. "Close to four hundred."

"Four hundred dollars? On footwear?"

"Just about."

"You people sure keep the white man rich then complain about being oppressed."

"Excuse me?"

"You know how many young punks I've arrested throughout the years for moving arms, and when we kick open the door to their dilapidated apartments, these kids have thirty-thousand-dollar Rolex watches, and dozens of sneakers piled up against their bedroom walls— enough sneakers to supply a whole African village—yet can't pay for a proper attorney?"

"So?"

"So?"

"Yeah, what right do you have to judge them? Or me for that matter?"

"Calm the fuck down and take that bass outta your voice. I'm just wondering, that's all."

"They buy what makes them feel better about themselves."

"Really? So those Prada sneakers are about self-esteem?"

"I buy Prada because I can. My self-esteem is already intact."

"You can afford four-hundred-dollar sneakers on your pay? Your pay grade is GS-level 4, Robertson. Who you foolin'?"

"I guess, not you." I cut my eyes toward James. I really wasn't sure where he was coming from. Perhaps the liquor was talking for him.

"Who the fuck cares about fashion? Huh? Not me." James gave me a playful punch on my shoulder with his massive fist. "However you get yours is your business. Fuck 'em! Fuck the government! Fuck the IRS! Fuck 'em all! Do you think I report all my earnings, my little side jobs, to Uncle Sam? Hell, fucking no!"

"I hear that," I replied, as the liquor finally began going to my head. "As you said, my pay grade don't stretch that far, so Uncle Sam don't know about half the shit I buy nor how I can afford it." I felt tipsy, but I wasn't drunk. I knew better than to open up to him about Dré and all the cocaine he was moving through Harlem.

"So what made you join the force?"

"Honestly, I needed a come-up. Something progressive that held respect."

"Respect?"

I shook my head and took another sip of Scotch, which burned going down. "Yeah, that was important."

"Do you mind telling me why?"

I hesitated briefly. "I dunno. I guess having a father in and out of 'club fed' all my life, a brother who's the dumbest criminal on earth, and a mother who has struggled with mental illness since I was born. I was always the butt of jokes where I grew up. But my environment and struggles actually helped propel me. It kept me ambitious and toughened me up. When I was twelve years old, I was fighting women twenty and up, all for respect."

"Didn't you grow up in Suffolk County?"

"Not at all. I grew up in East Harlem amongst prostitutes, pimps, and drug hustlers."

"Harlem?"

"Yeah, Harlem. And not the Harlem with the huge beautiful brownstones like the Huxtables lived in on *The Cosby Show*. I grew up in the gutter and had to claw my way out."

"Yeah, I had a hard life too. My old man used to beat the shit out of me on a regular basis, and my mother just sat there and let it happen." James had a faraway look in his eyes. "But the past is the past, right?"

"I hope so. I try not to let that shit get to me. It's all in how you cope with things. They can either break you or make you."

James held up the liter of Scotch. "This is how I cope with things."

"I think we should take it a little easy on that bottle, James."

James let out a hearty laugh, his deep blue eyes staring intently into mine. "You know, Honey, you really are beautiful."

"Thank you," I said and ran my hands through my short haircut.

"Do other black women think you're beautiful?"

"What type of question is that?"

"Do other people see what I see? Are your features considered beautiful to the blacks?"

I cocked my head to the side. *Did I hear him correctly?* "The blacks?"

"You know what I mean."

"No, no, the fuck I don't. You said it, not me."

"Calm down," James said assertively, almost bordering on a command.

"Ain't nobody hyped," I said, getting hyped.

James chuckled. "This ghetto hoochie-momma thing you got going is turning me the fuck on."

Taken aback by James' last comment, I instinctively looked down and noticed that he had unzipped his fly and was massaging his pink-colored penis.

"Come on and suck it," he said. "Give me what you give your husband."

Before I could react, James had his hand on the back of my neck, trying to lower my head.

"Get the fuck off me!" I knocked his hand away.

"Come on, just do it. Ain't nobody watchin'." James quickly peered over his shoulders. "Just suck me off, and I'll eat your pussy next. I promise."

Shell-shocked, all I could say was "Huh?"

Before I could think, I felt his strong hands groping and pulling at my clothes. His hands were fast and experienced, like he'd done this before. He leaned over and forced my seat back and already had half his body weight on top of me while his finger was close to being inserted into my pussy.

"Are you retarded?" I screamed. "Fuckin' psycho!"

James suddenly eased up, his blue eyes becoming small and menacing. "What did you call me, bitch?"

I stared at my supervisor and knew I had two choices. I didn't like either one, but I went with my gut. "I said, 'Get the fuck off me, psycho!'" and put my Glock 9 in his face. My clenched jaw felt like it would lock up. "Don't you ever put your filthy hands on me again!"

There was a stare down.

"You're fuckin' dead, you hear me? Dead!"

I managed to briefly see a little humor despite the tension. My supervisor was literally sitting with his dick in his hand and a gun in his face.

I backed out of the vehicle with my Glock steadied at his head. When I was clear, I hauled ass out of there and made my way home. I was too amped to be scared, yet I knew that things had boiled over. In a nanosecond things had changed. I went from being on a stakeout to catch a suspect moving weapons to almost getting raped by my supervisor.

I ran into my house like a tornado, only to be met by the sight of my husband, head first into some bitch's pussy. All I saw was dyed-red pussy hair and caramel-colored legs spread-eagled across my sofa. My heart sunk into my stomach. I knew at that moment what a broken heart felt like.

"What the fuck! Oh, hell no!" I could feel my body tense up, and I was rapidly losing control. The one person I trusted had betrayed me. "On our muthafuckin' couch, Dré? Seriously?!"

The red-haired-pussy bitch jumped up and quickly started scrambling and looking for her clothes.

"Baby, this ain't what you think," Dré said to me, standing to his feet. His dick was standing at attention and pointed right at me as he started to approach me with his hands in the air, showing surrender.

I pulled out my Glock and I aimed it right at his forehead. "Take one more step, and I'll blow your brains out!" My eyes cut to his mistress. "And tell that bitch to sit the fuck down right now!"

"Honey, why you—"

BLAOW!

I fired off one warning shot that whizzed right past Dré's head and lodged into the newly painted sheetrock wall in our living room. The shot had definitely caught everybody's attention.

"A'ight, baby, you win. I lose. I'm wrong, dead wrong," he said to me, his dick suddenly limp.

"So this is what you like?" I asked, my voice accusatory and laced with malice. My eyes scanned his chick from head to toe. I knew Dré was a street dude with a wandering eye when I married him, but you always think that your man wouldn't go there. It's always some other chick's man that's the tramp.

"Hell no, baby. I was just fuckin' her, that's all. It don't mean nothing."

"Dré, I know you're not going to stand there and tell her that I don't mean nothing to you," the chick said, rolling her eyes and looking at Dré.

Dré bent down and reached for his jeans.

"Did I tell you to get dressed?" I barked.

Dré looked at me like I was crazy and immediately dropped his jeans and let them hit the living room floor.

"Stand up," I said to the girl.

She sucked her teeth and stood up.

I saw the name Olivia tattooed on her left thigh. "You and your stripper bitch Olivia, march your asses downstairs right now."

"Stripper? Please." Olivia sucked her teeth again.

"You think I'm fuckin' playing games, bitch?" I was one second from whipping her ass. "Keep talking slick if you want to. Dré, you better school this ho if you want her to make it out of here alive."

Dré was heated on so many levels. No man wants to get caught fucking his side chick. Dré was busted and now to have me busting shots with my legal firearm was just too intense for him. He liked being in control, and standing butt-ass naked with nothing to defend himself with had aged him ten years. I could see the stress and worry written all over his face.

"Olivia, stop disrespecting my wife. Damn! How the fuck you think she feel right now?"

Olivia obliviously wasn't the silent type. Nor the sharpest knife in the drawer. Despite having used my pistol only moments earlier and still having it pointed at her head, she just couldn't police her mouth.

"Your wife? Nigga, you disrespect her each time we fuck! Each time you eat my pussy then kiss her lips you disrespect her!" Her voice elevated to a high pitch. "You never respected her, which allowed me to disrespect—"

Dré charged Olivia like a pro quarterback filled with rage and hostility and commenced to whipping her ass. His punches, heavy and overflowing with guilt and malice, landed on every exposed part of her body—head, stomach, back, thighs. Nothing was spared from his wrath. It all happened so quickly, I didn't have time to process what was happening. Yet, I didn't intervene. She needed her ass whipped for fucking another woman's husband in the apartment he shared with his wife. As a woman, she should have known better. Take that shit to a hotel; Dré could obviously afford a room.

I listened to Olivia scream for mercy until finally I got bored. No way was I going to allow Dré to erase his guilt by beating up his mistress in front of me.

"Knock it off, Dré!" I waited a few seconds and he didn't let up. The room was now warm from all the commotion and filled with unsavory body odors. Her exposed pussy coupled with being worked over had begun giving off a pungent odor that I didn't want any parts of. "I said knock it the fuck off!"

This time Dré fell back, breathing heavily and looking at Olivia in disgust, as if she was the culprit. "Don't cry now," he mocked. "Silly-ass bitch!"

"You two can take this lovers' quarrel elsewhere," I stated. "As I said, go the fuck downstairs. Now! Move your asses! And, if I have to say it again, I'ma start putting bulletholes in ankles, and you'll have to crawl the fuck downstairs!"

Dré shook his head and wanted to say something, but the glare in my eyes silenced his rebuttal. He grabbed the now battered and ego-bruised Olivia by the hand and almost dragged her out of our living room and down the one flight of stairs in our newly renovated brownstone apartment in Sugar Hill.

As I followed right behind them with my gun pointed at them, I peeped yet a second tattoo on Olivia. She had two cherries on her lower back. A tramp stamp is what I call tattoos placed in that spot.

"You on some bullshit, Dré!" Olivia said.

She definitely is defiant, I thought. I was two seconds from whacking that bitch upside her head with my gun.

When we made it to the bottom floor, I could tell that Dré was confused as to what was next.

"Now I want y'all both to get the fuck out," I said, raising my Glock and pointing it right at Olivia and Dré.

"Get the fuck out?" Dré asked.

"Open up that muthafuckin' door and get the fuck out, you and your little stripper freak."

"Honey, it's like zero below out this muthafucka!"

I cocked my gun to show Dré that I wasn't playing games. "I'm not negotiating shit. You was in my house disrespecting me with this whore, tramp bitch! So now we play by my rules. Open up that fuckin' door and walk the fuck out."

"I ain't got no fuckin' clothes on, Honey!"

"Do you seriously think I care about you? Either one of you? I have no sympathy for husbands who fuck on their wives!"

Dré wasn't moving, and neither was Olivia, so without hesitation I let off three consecutive shots right at them. Both of them began hopping up and down like something was hot under their feet. I was always on the gun range, so my aim was precise. I knew I wasn't going to hit them. I just wanted to get their respect. In the process, I was fucking up my crib, but with the way Olivia and Dré started scurrying and scrambling, it was worth it.

"Open that door and take your ass to Olivia's house and don't come the fuck back! Test me if you want to."

Olivia finally understood the seriousness of the situation. "Honey, honestly I—"

I screamed, "Bitch, why are you talking to me? Walk the fuck out that front door before I pop your ass! Are you stupid or what?"

She twisted her lips and walked over to the front door and opened it. Immediately a gust of frigid air burst through with a howling wind that could freeze your bones. Instantly Olivia and Dré wrapped their hands around their private parts and inched out the front door. Just as Dré got to the first exit step, I lifted my foot and, with all my strength, kicked him square in his ass. His body went face-first down a flight of steps and landed on the cold, hard concrete below.

Olivia, fearing the same fate, bolted down the steps on her own and ran full speed down the residential block, screaming at the top of her lungs, "She's crazy! She's crazy! She tried to kill us!"

I locked up the house and drove to my mother's. I needed time to think things through.

♠♠♠

"You're being suspended without pay until further notice. Please relinquish your gun and badge," our commanding chief, Inspector Balthazar Snashall stated. "Now."

"Why am I being punished?"

"You walked off the job during a stakeout, Robertson. Why do you think?"

I wanted so badly to tell what really happened, but I knew I wouldn't be believed. Not with five white smug faces sitting around the conference room. I looked at Dougherty and wondered what happened to him preaching about what occurred in the field staying in the field.

"But I didn't just walk off. Right, Dougherty?" My eyes cut to my left where his fat ass was propped up in an oversized leather chair. "I mean, I did give you notice. There was a *great* reason, right?"

"Fuck you," he said, words dragged out.

"That's exactly what you tried to do—Fuck me! You tried to rape me the other night, and that's why I left!"

The moment the words fell out my mouth, I knew I had fucked up. When the white faces got whiter, I knew there wasn't any way I could take them back.

"Gentlemen, will everyone excuse us," Inspector Balthazar said.

Everyone left the room glaring at me as I sat, hands trembling. I had so much at stake.

"Is that true? The rape allegation?"

"Yes, sir."

"Did you go to the hospital and get a rape kit done?"

"Well, no."

"Why not? You're a skilled agent."

"Well, it didn't get that far."

"You said rape. Isn't that far enough?"

"I said he tried to rape me. He obviously didn't succeed because, if he did, he wouldn't be breathing."

"Did you go to the local police and make out a report?"

"No, sir."

"Why not?"

"Well, because—"

"These are serious accusations, Robertson."

"With all due respect, sir, if you allow me to finish a sentence, I could tell you what happened."

"Honey, is Luther Brown your father?"

"Excuse me?"

"Luther Brown, he is your father, correct?"

"What does that have to do with anything?"

"What about Corey Atkinson, AKA Chief? Is he your half-brother? You two share the same mother?"

I began to experience a series of emotions that I couldn't control. I wrung my hands together, and they were damp.

"Look, sir, James Dougherty tried to rape me, and I think that I should be debriefed. All these other questions are secondary. My statement should be first."

"Are you telling me how to do my job?"

"I'm asking that you stay focused."

"I am focused. On your application . . . you do know lying on these applications is a federal offense punishable by law."

Now my heart was palpitating. How did I get here? "Yes, but—"

"Look, my time is valuable, and I'm not going to dick you around. Either resign today with two weeks' pay or face criminal sanctions."

"But I didn't do anything! What about Dougherty?" My plea almost sounded juvenile.

"How hypocritical are you? You lied on a federal application. Our agents put their lives in your hands when they go out on these raids, and the very people you're supposed to lock up are the very people you lied about having contact with. Your father is one of the most notorious illegal arms traffickers in the North, and your brother is a known drug-dealing pimp. You could have compromised several of our operations."

"I would never do that. I'm a good agent."

"You're just a baby. Hardly wet behind the ears. You don't know what it takes to be a good agent. It's all about the brotherhood and what you did, leaving your superior alone out in the field was incomprehensible."

"But—"

"There is no but! You need to grow up! In life we hardly get a do-over. You had your shot, and you blew it. You can't make a three-point shot from under the net, Honey. I've been doing this for years, so I think you should take my advice. Either resign and not have any blemishes on your record, or hold out for an investigation, and I promise what we'll dig up will prevent you from working an honest day's work in the government for the rest of your life."

The angst and anguish I felt began to boil over. A steady stream of tears began to flow freely. "But what about my mother? You know she needs my medical insurance. She's just started seeing a great psychiatrist. If I resign, I'll lose my health benefits."

Balthazar looked unaffected. "I'm going to step out of the room and give you time to think about your options."

I walked out of Pearl Street in lower Manhattan, the unknown address of the ATF, and barely got to my car. My world was crumbling under my feet. Just then two men in worn, inexpensive suits approached me.

Immediately I felt danger. *Could this be a hit?*

"Honey Robertson?"

"Yes?"

"Turn around and place your hands behind your back."

"What? Why?"

"You're under arrest for the attempted murder of André Robertson. You have the right to remain silent. Anything you say can and will be used against you . . ."

Chapter 1

I knew that the nine-hundred-dollar pair of Christian Louboutin's wasn't even supposed to be an afterthought, let alone a consideration. The red bottoms had caught my eye as I passed by the MAC counter in Neiman Marcus, taking a shortcut through the Bellagio Hotel on my way to work. I had been working as a blackjack dealer in the hotel for slightly over a year after I'd gotten fired from the federal government as an ATF agent. The Bureau was on some bullshit and got too hyped because I'd lied on my application, and coupled with the attempted murder rap, that was enough to get me out of town, and fast.

"Size eight, please," I said as I handed the display pair to the salesman. I then added, "You know what? Also bring out an eight and a half. Those shoes tend to be cut small."

I sat back calmly, with a watchful eye on two females I'd seen around the hotel on numerous occasions. They were get-money type chicks, always running some sort of hustle on some trick's pockets, jostling tourists, or selling tail.

The salesman came with both boxes, leaned down on one knee and opened up the size eight. He proceeded to place the shoe on my foot as if I were Cinderella, until I stopped him.

"I can do that," I said, and smiled slyly. "I bet you get a lot of numbers on your knees like that," I joked.

"You sound like my girl. Did she put you up to spying on me?"

"Here's a tip," I said then whispered, "If she's that insecure to have spies watching you, I'd drop her."

His eyes widened at the thought.

"No matter how good the pussy!"

I stood up with the size eight Louboutin's on and pranced to the mirror, loving the expensive piece of art on my foot. I then picked up two more displays and asked, "Could I see those as well?"

Eagerly the embarrassed salesman complied. He'd make a hefty commission if I actually bought the shoes. In Vegas, salesmen are used to women dropping large sums of cash on designer shoes. There was so much money trading hands in the casinos that this ordinary sales job was probably earning him more in one year's commissions than that of the previous jobs he'd held combined.

Before he knew it, I had him running in and out of the storeroom in a dizzying combination of small talk coupled with greed. His greed had clouded his judgment, and he was unaware that I had ordered twelve pairs of shoes but only gave him back eleven.

"You know what? I can't decide. They're all so beautiful. Are you working tomorrow?" I asked.

The once accommodating salesman now had a sour look plastered on his face and was less friendly. "I know you're not walking out of here without a pair of shoes after taking up all my time. I could have easily focused my attention on other customers."

Though I had stuffed a thousand-dollar pair of stilettos in my purse, I wanted to curse the greedy dude out but didn't want to cause too much of a scene.

"I really apologize, but I can't decide. OK, since you're pressuring me, did you like those on me?" I pointed toward the last pair the guy was still holding.

"These here were my favorites on you," he said. He glanced down at the price and was slightly heated that they only cost $675.00, a lower-end cost, but it sure beat a blank. He pushed, "Do you want to pay cash or charge?"

"Charge, please." I walked over to the counter and discreetly pulled out my wallet while fumbling inside to adjust the shoes. I slapped my plastic on the counter and waited.

"This card is declined. Do you have another one?"

"Declined?" My voice rose in a forced shock. "Try it again."

Once again the salesman tried to process the card. "Ma'am, this isn't working. Do you have cash?"

"Look, I'm late for work. I've been here long enough. Just place those on hold for me and I'll come back tomorrow with cash."

Still wanting to be hopeful that I would honor my word, he asked for my name.

"Honey. Honey Brown."

Confidently, I walked toward the front door and into the loud, obnoxious sounds of Las Vegas. The slot machines annoyed the hell out of me. But everything I hated about Vegas was everything that would assist me with my master plan.

I slipped on my new six-inch stilettos—the shoes were my favorite color of money green, which dressed up my normal black slacks and Bellagio uniform top. Everyone knew that I always tried to sexy up the place. My short haircut was always styled, nails done, shoes game tight, hourglass figure toned, and bank account on *E*. I'd lost everything I had, including my life savings, fighting the allegations the government had lodged against me, and the trumped-up attempted murder beef my ex-husband eventually dropped. By the time it was all over, I owed more than a hundred grand on my credit cards and had spent nearly fifteen thousand dollars on attorney fees. I came to Las Vegas on a one-way ticket, with six hundred dollars in cash, and a plan that would set me up for life.

I walked over to Carlos, who I would be relieving from his shift.

"How did everything go on your shift?" Not that I truly cared, but it was easier to blend in if you didn't seem standoffish.

"I killed them, Honey! There was this couple that tried to take the house for twenty-five grand. The husband and wife were pros. We had the new girl, Samantha, shuffling. I tapped in and relieved her, and it was downhill from there. Once they were wiped out of the twenty-five grand they were up, the husband went and brought another ten grand to the table, and I brought all that home. He was so mad, he accused me of cheating and had to be escorted out. Dumb ass! Everyone knows the house always wins."

To hear the enthusiasm in Carlos' voice was disturbing. I mean, who was the real dumb ass? He was getting excited over money that wasn't his. He was making ten bucks an hour and talking like he was co-owner of the Bellagio. One day he'll wake up and realize that him taking his job personally wasn't worth it. Not one supervisor, manager, co-owner, or owner really gave a fuck. It was only business. And if the Bellagio had to make a choice today to fire his Mexican ass to adjust their bottom line, they wouldn't give a damn about how loyal a blackjack dealer he was. Me, I didn't give a fuck who was up or down. I shuffled the cards, made small talk, and kept it moving. I was in Vegas for one thing, and one thing only.

♠♠♠

What I liked about Vegas was that it seemed like you could work almost anywhere and still be able to afford a house or a really nice apartment for little money. Everyone I had met since moving out to Las Vegas was always telling me how bad the city had been hit by the recession. And apparently the recession had caused housing prices and apartment rental prices to hit rock bottom owing to hundreds of thousands of foreclosures.

I didn't want to get locked into a mortgage, but at the same time I didn't want to live in a small cramped apartment either. So what I did was, I found the best of both worlds and ended up renting a huge apartment about ten miles or so from the Vegas strip. But the apartment complex had all of the amenities that I liked and felt that I needed. It had a gym where I could workout, a pool, and nice patio areas where I could barbecue and entertain company and simply lay out in the sun if I so chose.

It seemed like a lot of people in Vegas weren't too big on barbecuing, maybe because it's so damn hot all of the time, but barbecuing was something I loved to do when I was in New York and did often at my apartment in Vegas.

Today I found myself with a charcoal grill full of Italian sausages, hot dogs, hamburgers, ribs, and corn. I loved to have company and entertain people, and I liked to cook, so needless to say, my house was a revolving door with my friends and, on occasion, my single boo Stephon, and on very, very rare occasions with my married booty-call boo, Brian.

At my apartment were Mercedes, Party, and Natasha. We ate good food and drank liquor, while Mercedes and Party smoked their weed. I'd never had all three girls together at the same time, but we weren't there just to hang out. We were there to finalize the heist.

"Remember this, if nothing else. Have it etched in your brains. No cell phones! They track by the cell towers, and if anyone gets knocked and rolls over, they'll pull our cell records to tell our story. Our phones will corroborate a snitch's claim. They'll be able to connect the dots before, during, and after the robbery. Capiche?" I flipped a slab of ribs.

"We hear you, Honey," Party said. "Everyone will check their purses, cars, jeans—the whole nine—to make sure we're not ridin' dirty."

I nodded my approval.

"Honey, there is something that's not sitting right with me." Party sipped on her Hennessy, which she always drank straight.

"What's up?"

"I just get this gut feeling that we need to fallback off the whole thing and wait maybe six months to a year."

"Six months to a year? What are you talking about, Party? You know something that we don't know?"

"It's the whole cell phone thing. I mean, of course, we won't use our phones to communicate, but it's not like me and you just met. We been knowing each other for like a year or better now," Party said.

"Yeah. And your point is?"

"My point is just what you said. If one of us gets knocked, then they are going to check records and they'll know who we was talking to. But the fact that we called each other even once, that in itself could be the thing that does us in. And why wouldn't they just go back and check those records and connect the dots that way?"

Party had a damn good point, and it was something that I sort of overlooked. At the same time, I wasn't too worried, because I had long since gotten rid of my old cell phone, as did Party, and for the past few months, we had all been using prepaid cell phones.

"I just think if we waited it helps us avoid any chance that some smart-ass cop could connect us in any way."

Party was on that "weed intellect." Whenever she smoked, she'd get paranoid and start to overthink.

"Party, you just scared," Mercedes said. "Honey, she ain't built for this. She already having cold feet. So if she does get bagged, you know she's going to run her mouth."

"Mercedes, what are you talking about?" Party said with an attitude. "Ain't no way I'd ever turn snitch. Honey, you know me, and I handle mines. And I know you're the brains behind this complex operation, but even the president has a vice-president to catch what he might miss. You feel me? I just want us to do what no other has done, which is get away with successfully robbing the Bellagio Casino."

"Mercedes, Party is right, and that's how we all need to be thinking. We have to think past the obvious so that we don't get tripped up by not being as thorough as we could be. Believe me, I've thought this plan through one thousand ways and it's solid. As long as we stay on our A-game and foresee the unforeseen, the money is already ours. All we have to do is take it."

Mercedes looked at me and nodded her head, but she didn't say anything to Party.

I continued, "And please don't make me keep repeating this⊠Stay out of the casinos, from today moving forward, at least until we've successfully pulled off this heist. I don't want anyone remembering faces, body language, voices, nothing. The smallest detail can be remembered by a potential witness." I stared directly at Natasha, who tossed her eyes toward the sky. "Natasha, I'm speaking to you too."

"Why am I being singled out? Mercedes and Party like to gamble too. And you work there."

"Mercedes and Party don't have an addiction, so if I say stay away, they will. You, on the other hand, might be a problem." I hardened my voice. "And as for me, as you said, I work there. So how the fuck can I stay away? I'm the inside connect, remember?"

"Honey, we feel you, and it's not a problem to stay away. But in Vegas that's what people do, and our avoiding the casinos could be a red flag and actually draw attention to us then reflect it," Party added.

"If you're invited by a third party, then by all means go. But the real point is, don't make it your home away from home. Casino security and the dealers are taught to be observant. We're taught to remember what brand of cigarettes a player was smoking."

"OK, understood. We all agree that we'll only go to the casinos under relevant circumstances."

Everyone said in unison, "Agreed."

"So let's go over the plan one more time," I stated.

I had the blueprints of the Bellagio Hotel and Casino, a map covering the north and south radius of the Las Vegas strip and each entrance and exit of each highway. A police scanner stayed on during each meeting, and we all had custom-molded Bluetooth earpieces, the surveillance device that the Secret Service uses to communicate. It would allow each of us to speak to one another before, during, and after the heist. Old-school and inexperienced criminals would use outdated, bulky, walkie-talkies with a four-second delay in response time. That four seconds could cost either one of us our life. The invisible Bluetooth earpiece would allow us to operate in real-time, leaving no room for error.

"We have to be on point with everything. Y'all gotta remember, a heist consists of three parts: the plan, the execution, and the getaway. Who's gonna run down protocol?"

Mercedes spoke first. "At around eight fifteen a.m.—"

"Mercedes, no! How many times do I have to stress punctuality? It's approximately eight thirteen a.m. Eight fuckin' thirteen! It's that exact. They run their operation down to the last second. You gotta feel me on that, babe. If not, we're all going away for a long time, and I don't mean Disneyland."

We'd been over this plan for the past nine months day in and day out, and still Mercedes was speaking in hypotheticals.

"I'm sorry, Honey."

"Don't be sorry, be exact!"

"OK, you're right. At approximately eight thirteen a.m., the Brinks truck will leave its central station carrying"—she paused before adding—"seventy million dollars in unmarked US currency. There will be exactly three guards: the driver, the principal guard riding shotgun, and the backup riding in the back bin with all the dough. The armored truck will be heading south on Interstate 15 and will take approximately ten minutes to reach South Las Vegas Boulevard, the exit to the Bellagio. From that exit it will take the armored car nine minutes on the busy Las Vegas strip to arrive at the back entrance of the casino, where two more armed guards will assist them with the exchanging of the monies."

"Party, that's where you come in," I said as I looked at her.

Party was "my right-hand man." Though she was of average height and weight, underneath her clothes were all muscle. She'd been in and out of "juvie" since she was thirteen and had done a stint in Bedford Hills Correctional Facility for Women in upstate New York. She was pretty in an androgynous sort of way. She wore a sleek bob haircut and Chuck Taylor kicks and had the largest feet I'd ever seen on a female, sporting a size eleven in men's sneakers. But she was good peoples. Her jeans were always pulled low, yet she coupled that with tight-fitting tank tops with her massive double Ds spilling over. Men didn't hesitate to do a double take, and women looked too. Her voice was raspy, and her attitude gruff. A biracial mix of Black and Asian, she was as hardcore as they come.

"Dressed disguised as a male and as the hotel's cleaning service, at approximately eight thirty-three a.m., exactly one minute after the truck arrives, I'll begin inching my way toward the driver with my TEC-9 hidden discreetly under my oversized uniform shirt."

"Now this is where Mercedes and I get busy. At approximately eight thirty-four a.m., we will both make our way toward the armored truck and the guards. It will only take the guard handling the money a few seconds to realize we're not the normal exchange team. That team will have already been apprehended and permanently put out of commission with one shot to the dome at exactly eight twenty-five by us. He may engage us in small talk, he may not. He may automatically try to retreat or signal his backup."

"At that point, I pull out my AK and put it in the driver's face and say, 'If you move, muthafucka, my gat gonna blow your fuckin' back out!'" Party simulated her move as if she was really in the middle of the heist.

"Cool. Mercedes you and I will already have the drop on the two guards. We now have seven minutes before people begin getting antsy and stragglers begin rolling in for their shift change. The casino's back entrance will be crowded with employees changing shifts. That's a double-edged sword. More people will ensure more confusion, but it will also give more witnesses. So we want people to shield us from the guards, but we don't want them to remember us. From when the guard gets out of the truck, it takes approximately eight minutes to go in the back and collect the receipts, drop off the money, and return back to the truck. We're intervening at two and a half minutes. Mercedes, I'll have your back, and, Party, you'll have all of our backs. Mercedes, as soon as the guard is ten meters from the truck, you walk right up to him and blow his muthafuckin' brains out. Put one in his head, and that'll make everyone scatter. But remember, and this is for all of us, Do not put more than one bullet in any organ. You can take one kill-shot in the head, or one kill-shot in the heart—"

"You keep reminding us of that but you never tell us why?" Mercedes stated.

In my training we're taught to double tap—two shots with rapid succession to the head or heart in close proximity. Then you reexamine your target and see if they are still a threat. I don't want the cops being tipped off that the mastermind is someone who was formerly in law enforcement.

"I keep reminding everyone because it's important. We all are either trained or been training to shoot with precision. The average criminal can't pull off such accuracy and once the investigation gets underway regarding the heist, the last thing I want is for the police to narrow their list of suspects. We don't want to be sloppy but we want to appear sloppy, almost amateurish if possible to throw them off our trail. Does that make sense to anyone?"

Everyone nodded.

"Good. Now back to Mercedes. You'll hit the guard once in the dome and before he can even hit the floor, I'm all over the bags of dough. Party . . ."

"Yes, sir."

"As soon as the guard inside the truck hears the shot he's going to come out trying to blaze, if he has any heart. If he doesn't, he'll take cover inside the truck and try to knock me off and Mercedes through the gun port or air vents in the truck. You need to be fast like lightning and take care of him either way. If he opens that door, you aim for either his knees or preferably above the neck. He'll be wearing a bulletproof vest, so your aim from a distance needs to be accurate. If he tries to run out the passenger side of the truck, he'll have a blindside. Remember what I said—Drop to the ground and shoot out his ankles. You'll only have seconds to run around to the other side of the armored truck and finish him off.

"Meanwhile, we have to secure three guards, grab the money, and make a clean getaway all within thirteen minutes. Natasha, that's where you come in. You'll pull the throwaway car about a hundred and fifty feet behind the truck—"

"What type of ride will be the throwaway?"

"Why does that matter? It'll be whatever we lift two days before the heist."

"It matters because I need to envision this step by step, and if I know what type of ride we gonna boost—"

"Natasha, please. Seriously, each meeting you find a way to work someone's nerves. Not today, please. Let's just stay focused. You can envision a Ford Taurus, OK."

"OK, Honey. Ford Taurus . . . that works."

"Cool. Now you will have to get us to the highway in six minutes, no matter what. You feel me? Whoever isn't in that getaway car gets left out there on that strip. And that includes me."

"I gotchu, bossy. I know these Vegas streets like the back of my hands. Nobody can fuck with me when I'm behind the wheel."

Natasha claimed she was Russian, but she didn't have a hint of an accent. No one believed her. She was tall with bleach-blonde hair and plain features. She wasn't a beauty, nor was she the bottom of someone's shoe. She was a'ight. But I didn't commission these women for their looks nor their brains. They all got hired for their hearts. It was going to take a lot of heart to pull off what we were attempting to pull off. When I did a background check on each girl, I found out that each one had done something so outlandish, it piqued my interest. Since they were caught they were labeled fools, but had they gotten away with it, they would have been considered masterminds.

"Good to hear."

"But, Honey?"

"What's up, Party?"

"I know we've been over this hundreds of times—"

"Thousands."

"Yeah, thousands. But I can't shake that I feel we need a fifth girl. Extra muscle out there while we're holding down the guards and also packing up the money. I got this eerie feeling that one or all of the guards will try us. We need an extra set of eyes and hands out there."

"Nah, four mouths to feed is enough," Mercedes spat. "We already gotta split the money equally with Natasha, and she ain't even doing shit."

Mercedes was the only one who had children. She had two little girls, and that bothered me. She was Mexican with a large, poor family that immigrated to the United States. Her first baby daddy split before the child was born, and the second was murdered during a drug deal gone wrong.

Mercedes and Jesus had tried to setup and rob a local drug dealer. Only, he opened fire first, and she was shot in her knee. The bullet went in and out, and she never sought medical attention. Her grandmother sewed up the wound, and she handled her pain by tossing back Tylenol extra strength. Jesus wasn't so lucky. His brains were scattered on Biscayne Boulevard in Miami. She immediately had to leave and moved out West to start over. While out in Vegas she honed her skills as a computer hacker and did small white collar crimes; stealing credit card numbers, emptying small bank accounts, and identity theft to pay her bills.

"I beg your pardon?" Natasha stated, a quizzical look on her face.

"Oh, fuck you with that proper shit," Party said. "Bitch, you grew up in the hood just like the rest of us. You're the only one who ain't gettin' dirty. You sittin' in a nice secure car, while we're all out here risking our lives, but yet you gonna get the same reward as me, Honey, and Mercedes?"

The room imploded in anarchy. I didn't immediately interrupt because I knew the pent-up emotions needed to be let out. We had less than two weeks before we made our attempt to get that dirty money, so I was sure everyone's nerves were frayed.

Finally, I yelled, "Quiet!" and the room hushed to a whisper.

"Party, I know you and Mercedes might think that Natasha's role is inconsequential, but it's not. Taking the money will be like taking candy from a baby. We'll have home-court advantage, and they will be taken by surprise. Why do you think we're doing the heist on a Wednesday and not a Friday when the till would be double? It's because Monday through Wednesday the guards on duty are soft like marshmallow.

I've pulled their backgrounds and profiled them. Neither one of those guards are prone to violence. They won't try to play hero. Trust me.

"The most difficult part of the heist is the getaway. What if—and this is only pure speculation to help bring this situation to closure—the cops get the chase on us? Who would you rather behind the wheel, huh? Me? You? Mercedes?" I waited for a response, but Party just grunted.

"Exactly. You'd want Natasha. Now I gets busy on a motorcycle, but four wheels has never been my thing. And the only way to have full cooperation and a willing participant is if you even the playing field. Now that Natasha will have equal vested interest in the heist, she will equally want to get away with it. Understood?"

Party reluctantly nodded.

"Good. Now that was criminology 101. I hope you enjoyed your free lesson."

Chapter 2

I was cuddled up next to my boo Stephon. We were laying in my bed after a half-hour of good sex. The central air was on, and it was helping to cool off the heat that we had generated while fucking.

"I love fuckin' you, baby." I kissed him on the cheek, and then I gave him a peck on his chest.

"You already know how I feel."

"Yeah, I do! You little bitch!" I jokingly said, elbowing him in the ribs.

"What was that for?"

"For your comment from two days ago when you said I was in your top three of all time sex partners."

"What's wrong with that?"

"*Helloooo*, I should be number one, not just in the top three. Punk ass!"

Stephon chuckled. "See, if I told you that you were number one and that your pussy was the best I ever had, then you wouldn't stay on top of your game. Competition brings out the best in everybody."

"Competition? Nigga, I'll cut your dick off if you fuckin' somebody else." I grabbed him by his balls.

"Ahh shit! Chill, chill. That's not what I was trying to say." Stephon laughed and grimaced at the same time as he tried to explain himself. "See, your pussy is the best, but I have to tell you that it's in the top three because, if I said it was the best, you wouldn't have no motivation to do all them little pussy-tightening tricks that you do when we're fucking."

I looked at Stephon with playful suspicion. "Um, hmmm."

At that moment my phone started to ring. I looked at the caller ID and realized that it was my dad. I already knew what he wanted, so I was hesitant to pick up the phone. Not to mention, speaking to my dad was totally going to fuck up the lovey-dovey mood that me and Stephon was enjoying.

Eventually I answered and had to listen to my father's slick talk. I wasn't quite sure how I felt about his insisting that he fly out West. He and I hadn't been on the best terms since my mother took her own life. At first I'd blamed everyone. Now I only blamed one.

"Your old man don't have nowhere else to go, Honey. And I'm not taking no for an answer. I'm your father. I brought you in this world, and I can take you out!"

My father was always using those old-school terms that, as a child, intimidated me. As an adult, they were very comical.

"Daddy, I wasn't saying no. I was saying not right now."

"Those word games don't work on your old man. I put you through the school of manipulation. Now I need to be on the next thing smoking."

"Where are you?"

"I'm at your Aunt Betty's house. I swear, between her funky-ass feet and her loud cackling, I'm one day away from putting my foot up her ass!"

"How you gonna threaten your sister and you're living under her roof?"

"Her roof? This your roof. And every other taxpayer who's footing the bill. I swear, if I was in office, I'd do away with all that welfare, Section 8, unemployment, disability bullshit! It would all have to go. All it does and has done is handicap a whole race. Just genocide to keep them trapped in a labyrinth of poverty, drugs, and black-on-black crime."

I listened to my father's hypocrisy. He was a sketchy man with shifty eyes. Back in his day he terrorized a whole neighborhood.

"Well, you've had your hand in black-on-black crime, and let's not go there about taxpayers' dollars, when you never worked an honest job in your life."

"See? There you go. I paid my debt to society. Besides, this isn't about me."

"It never is."

"I know I don't hear any sarcasm coming out your mouth."

I wasn't about to be baited into an argument. "I'll have a ticket waiting for you at JFK Airport on Sunday. I'll call you and give you the details."

"So I guess there wasn't any sarcasm?"

We both laughed.

"You always have to have the last word," I said, matter-of-factly.

"That's what bosses do."

We hung up, and I redirected my attention back to Stephon.

"So, you're making arrangements for your father to come?"

I rolled my eyes. "If you couldn't tell, he forced his way here."

"He shouldn't have to force himself on his daughter."

"I hope you're not judging me." I sat up straight in bed, no longer wanting to cuddle. "You don't know my family like I do."

"But I want to get to know them, Honey." Stephon rubbed my cheek with his hand gently. "They're an extension of you, and I want to know everything about you."

"Babe, I swear I don't know if you're ready for this level of dysfunction."

"Actually, I love family dysfunction. My family was so straight-laced and boring, it's like a breath of fresh air," Stephon replied.

"Yeah, you say that now, but you haven't met my gangster-ass father and ghetto-ass brother yet."

"So they still coming out here?"

"Unfortunately, yes, they are."

Stephon had no idea why my brother was coming out to Vegas to see me, and he also had no idea about the get-money plot I was planning on pulling off.

♠♠♠

See, truth be told, Stephon was the last type of dude I thought I would end up with. That was because he and I came from two completely different worlds. Stephon was from a two-parent household and had grown up in the Las Vegas suburbs with all kinds of stability and shielding from the horrors of life. What he experienced was the exact and complete opposite of what I had experienced.

Where I grew up sort of shaped the type of dudes I was attracted to. Even though I had been with Dré from my teenage years, I had always been attracted to the rough, bad-boy, hustler type dudes. I think it was because, to me, those type of dudes represented strength, protection, and a form of financial stability, all of which made me feel secure in a womanly kind of way.

Stephon was as attractive as they come. He was light-skinned, with perfect waves, and he had a nice body with the six-pack to match. Everything about Stephon screamed pretty boy. Nothing about him screamed hustler or roughneck, and that was the only thing about him that had turned me off in the beginning when I first met him.

Fortunately for me, I had decided to give Stephon a play, and I gave him my number even though his rap was real weak in my opinion. I still laughed to myself at times when I thought back to when and how I'd first met him. I was heading in to work at the Bellagio when I saw a stretch Hummer limo parked in front of the hotel, which was a pretty common sight in Vegas. Only, this time the driver was trying to holler at me.

"Excuse me, can I talk to you for a moment?" Stephon had said to me as I walked briskly past him. He was dressed in a single-breasted black suit with a white shirt and skinny black necktie, looking like the epitome of lame.

"I'm sorry, but I'm really in a hurry," I said courteously.

"Two minutes, that's all I want," Stephon said, holding up two fingers and giving me a look like a child begging for a Happy Meal or something.

I shook my head, and I blew some air from my lungs as I stopped in my tracks.

Stephon smiled and approached me. "I guess I made myself look pretty obvious."

I was totally confused, and my face showed it. I asked him, "What are you talking about?"

"The way I be staring at you when I always see you," he replied.

"Me?"

Stephon nodded his head.

"Really? Well, actually, I never seen you before in my life, but like I was saying, I really have to go, and your two minutes are up."

Stephon knew that he was cute and with his pretty-boy look he was coming across as if he was God's gift to women. I knew I had deflated his ego, but that wasn't what I was even trying to do. All I was doing was being honest. And the truth was, he may have noticed me in the past, but I really didn't remember ever seeing him at all.

Stephon asked the obvious after looking at my name tag and uniform. "So, Honey, you work for the Bellagio?"

"Yes, I do. Listen, can we cut to the chase. I don't give out my number, but give me yours, and I'll call you in a couple of days. But I really have to bounce, or I'm gonna be late."

Stephon nodded his head. He reached into his pocket for a business card and handed it to me.

"OK, Stephon?" I asked after reading his card.

"Yes, you pronounced it correct. I own the company, so you can call me at anytime."

I nodded my head as I looked at Stephon. I could tell that he expected me to just be so blown away and impressed by the fact that he owned a limo company, but I wasn't.

There was about fifteen seconds of awkward silence, and then I stuck out my hand and told him that it was nice to meet him, that I would call him, and I walked off.

♠♠♠

"Ha ha ha ha ha!" I got up from the bed and prepared to go into the kitchen to cook some food.

Stephon asked me, "What's so funny?"

"I was just thinking about how weak your game was when we first met and how corny you were," I said in a non-hurtful way.

"Yeah, but fast-forward six weeks after that and I was tapping that ass."

"Fuck you." I smiled and walked out of the room.

"I make you rain, baby. Admit it. Let me hear you admit that shit," Stephon jokingly yelled from the room.

The truth was, he definitely did know how to fuck me the way I liked to be fucked. But aside from the sex, it was so hard for me to explain how I ended up falling for him the way I did. Stephon's parents were Haitian, so I always teased him, telling him that he must have put a spell of Haitian voodoo on me or something.

As it turned out, I did like the fact that Stephon was an entrepreneur. Although he only had one limo in his company, he did have the drive and ambition to make it. I knew that eventually he was going to build his company to the point where he had a huge fleet of limos and drivers.

And if things were to work out the way I hoped, Stephon didn't know it, but I was planning on hitting him off with the money he needed to purchase the fleet of limos he needed to take him to the next level.

My baby worked way too hard and worked all kinds of crazy hours trying to make it, so I was definitely going to get him up from under that daily grind as soon as I pulled off the crime of the century.

♠♠♠

The hot Nevada sun beat down on my back. The spaghetti strap T-shirt was an open invitation to sunburn. I was pacing back and forth on the sidewalk of McCarran International Airport waiting for my father's flight to arrive. I had mixed emotions about his arrival. I was smack-dab in the middle of negotiating and masterminding the biggest heist in the history of Las Vegas. And although I knew my dad would be down for whatever, I also didn't need any distractions. My father had high highs and low lows, not to mention an addiction.

"Little Bit!"

I immediately spun around. Any icicles I had around my heart immediately melted. I hadn't heard that nickname in years.

"Come give your old man a hug."

With arms gaping, I enveloped myself into his warm embrace and was accosted by Rémy Martin.

He was all juiced up and obviously feeling good. "So what's really good out here?"

"Whatever your pleasure. Most people get caught up in the casinos either because they're amateur or professional gamblers, or they work the casino like I do. I'm a blackjack dealer."

"Come off it, Honey. You think I had you fly me halfway around the world to hear you talk about blackjack?"

We walked toward my parked car and got in. "Dad, you flew five hours. Why do you always have to exaggerate?"

"You know what I mean. I keep telling you to stop being so literal.

I have to always exaggerate and also think outside the box. It keeps you one step ahead of the game. Had you listened to your old man's advice, it would not have gone down the way it did with the ATF."

That acronym still had the power to make me cringe.

"Let's not go there, OK."

"Still salty?"

"Wouldn't you be?"

"Fuck it. It's the past. You can't rewrite history, but you can write your future. You wrote the blueprint to how it went down when you opened the floodgates of your big mouth. Had you not confided in that dude about me and your brother, he would not have had the ammunition needed to fuck you over. And I'm not talkin' about the attempted sexual assault. Didn't I always tell you real bosses move in silence?"

"I don't know what got into me. He had just made me feel comfortable enough to open up."

"Honey, everyone has a predatory muscle, as everyone has a weakness. Your weakness exposed his predatory muscle."

I shifted in my seat, still seething from not exacting revenge. Because I lost my job, I could no longer pay for my mother's medical. The insurance company dropped me, and I was no longer able to pay for her to get the treatment she needed. It didn't take long for her to go off her meds, slit her wrist, and take a permanent nap. The depression coupled with psychosis was too much for anyone to handle alone.

"But it's not all bad though," I exclaimed. "I actually learned so much from not only that incident but also from my training at the ATF. Invaluable information that one day I will put to good use."

"Now we've come full circle."

"We have?"

"Why the fuck did you send for your brother? Whatever you two got planned, I want in."

Chapter 3

Chief sat in his sister's apartment with his feet perched on her coffee table. His dirty Tims had seen better days. He was sporting a pair of oversized Sean John jeans and no shirt. His hairy chest, tattered with bulletholes wasn't an appealing sight. There was a half-pound of weed on a plate, not for resale but for his pleasure. Two spliffs were cut and ready to be filled to the brim with purple haze and a bottle of Hennessy barely had a swallow left. Pumpkin, some random chick he picked up at the Wynn Hotel and Casino, was buttnaked. She had fucked him all morning and was patiently waiting to get paid. Sundays were usually slow, so she didn't mind allowing the clock to tick on just one john.

Chief had moves to make and needed a quick come-up, so when his sister called, he didn't think twice about leaving New York. Honey couldn't really talk over the telephone, but he knew that she'd better make his dropping everything to come to Vegas worth it. She'd sent him the cash to take a flight via Western Union, but his goon squad—Big Meech and Delano—had to take the Greyhound bus out West. They were pissed, but Chief explained they had to charge that to the game.

"Yo, what time you getting up outta here?" Chief asked, suddenly bored with the country chick.

Pumpkin was trying to throw in another blowjob or a quickie to increase her fee. Although she never got attached to a trick, he did have some good dick. "What's the rush, baby?" she purred, reaching for his dick.

Chief smacked her hand away. "Stop! And get up and put some clothes on. It's damn near three o'clock in the afternoon and you're still up in here butt-ass naked."

Pumpkin didn't like the shift in his mood, but she was used to erratic behavior from her tricks. "I just want to know where you got to be that's better than right here with me."

Chief stood up and hovered over the petite, fragile Pumpkin. "Are you questioning me, bitch?"

"No, no, not at all, baby. I just wanted to make you feel good."

"First off, I ain't your baby. I'm a grown-ass man. Don't be running that tramp talk like I'm some lame muthafucka who don't get pussy."

Pumpkin began biting her bottom lip. Her eyes cut to her Marc Jacobs bag, where she held her .380.

Chief walked toward her purse. "Oh, you want this?" It was heavy, and immediately he knew what was up. Inside he found her Smith & Wesson gun. Instantly he was filled with rage. He quickly pulled out on her, and Pumpkin knew she was in deep shit.

"You were trying to set me up, bitch?"

"Set you up? What are you talkin—"

The backhand slap with the large ring on his finger silenced the stunned Pumpkin. Her hands immediately went up to shield herself from further blows. Thick blood oozed out of her wound, and she knew the injury would surely scar and leave a mark. She was pissed.

"Oh, you ain't got shit to say now, right? Huh?" Chief towered over the trembling woman. "You think a nigga like me don't got the baddest chicks waiting on me back home?"

Pumpkin took a deep breath and exhaled. She needed to regain control of the situation before it went too far. "I know you do, big daddy. That's why I wanted to spend as much time with you as possible and didn't want to share your good lovin' with anyone else."

Chief didn't hesitate to smash his fist into her jaw. He punched on the woman like he was fighting a dude in the streets, her lean body taking blow after blow of his indescribable fury. Seconds felt like days to the helpless Pumpkin. All she could do was ball her body up into the fetal position and try her best to protect her head and face. Eventually the blows slowed down to a halt.

"Look what you made me do!" Chief barked. "Done fucked up my Tims and everything wit' your blood. I should make you clean all this shit up!" He grabbed Pumpkin up by her arm like a rag doll and tossed her off the sofa. "Go in the kitchen and get something to clean up this mess!"

The still defiant Pumpkin wanted no parts in the cleanup. "Just give me my money, so I can leave. You done had your fun with me. Now playtime is over!" she said, her breasts heaving up and down from fear and anger.

Chief's laughter was high-pitched and maniacal. "You thought I was gonna pay for your wack-ass pussy?" He emptied the contents of her purse onto the table and grabbed her wallet. "No, bitch. You're gonna pay for this good dick. Isn't that what you said? That I had some good lovin'. Well, let's see, I charge"—He counted all her cash—"two hundred and forty-seven dollars for this good lovin'. And you're lucky, because that's my discounted rate."

Pumpkin smirked at his audacity and watched as Chief stuffed all of her money into his pocket and seemed to be proud of his antics.

"You sick bastard!" Pumpkin yelled in anguish.

Chief pulled out his pistol from his waistband and stuffed it into Pumpkin's mouth. Every inch of her body trembled. Although she knew that selling tail could put her in a precarious situation, she thought she was smarter than the average prostitute, that she could spot a psycho a mile away.

They stared eye to eye.

"I'm gonna pull it," Chief stated, his face twisted up in anger. He looked demonic, almost monstrous.

Pumpkin squinted her eyes and braced for it. Seconds felt like years, numerous thoughts flooding her mind.

"Don't cry now," he replied, and ejected his gat.

Pumpkin flopped back down on the sofa and began bawling her eyes out. Chief lit up a spliff to take the edge off and thought about fucking her one more time before kicking her out for good.

"What the fuck!" He lunged toward Pumpkin and snatched the telephone receiver out of her hands, but it was already too late.

Seconds later the telephone rang. Chief took out his pistol and steadied it on Pumpkin. His look alone silenced her.

"Yes, hello."

"Sir, this is the nine-one-one operator. We just got a call, and someone hung up. Is everyone all right?"

"Yes, ma'am. My son was playing with the telephone, but his mother has him now."

"You're sure everyone is OK in there?"

"Yes, ma'am. We're all OK. We're just about to sit down and have supper."

"OK, thank you, sir."

"You're welcome," Chief sang and hung up. "You're wrong for that one, bitch!" As Chief inched closer to the terrified Pumpkin, he heard the jangling of keys at the door.

Seconds later Honey entered with her father.

"What the fuck is going on?" Honey asked, shock plastered on her face.

Pumpkin was confused. Could Honey be one of the 'baddest chicks' Chief was referring to earlier? Was this chocolate beauty his girlfriend? Pumpkin didn't know if she also had to defend herself against this female, and if so, she was spent. She couldn't take another beatdown.

"This ain't how it seems, Honey. You and Dad just go in your room and let me handle this."

"Like the fuck we will," Luther said. He could never stand Chief and not because he wasn't his biological son. Chief was a loser to Luther and could never quite master the game, no matter how many times Luther had tried to school him. "How many times we done told you about putting your hands on a woman?"

Once Pumpkin realized Honey and Luther were kin to Chief and were against his actions, she ran and embraced Honey. "P-p-p-please help me. He's crazy!" she yelled, stark naked and shivering.

"Shhhhh. It's gonna be OK." Honey rubbed her shoulders. "Go and put your clothes back on."

Pumpkin ran and began gathering her clothes when a loud banging on the door interrupted everyone. From the hard pounding on the door and the worried expression on Chief's face, everyone knew it was five-O.

"Who?"

"Police!"

Honey motioned for Chief to take the girl into the back room and hide, to which he was only too happy to oblige. He held her mouth tight and dragged her into the bedroom closet. Just as they were about to pound again Honey swung open the door.

"Ma'am, we got a distress call ten minutes ago. That's when—"

"Someone called the dispatcher and hung up."

"Correct," the officer said, his head cocked to the side. "Has this happened to you in the past?"

"No, sir. I'm just familiar with protocol, from my training."

"Oh, you're on the force?"

"ATF, New York division," she lied.

"Well, I'm glad to make your acquaintance. Might I ask, what are you doing so far away from home? Are you on a case?"

Honey knew he was trying to trip her up. "If I were I wouldn't be able to disclose that to you. But you already knew that, correct?"

He laughed. "I guess that's true. So why are you here?"

"I'm visiting. This is my father, Luther. He just picked me up from the airport, and I plan to spend my two-week vacation cleaning out your casinos of all its cash." Honey laughed at the irony, because that was exactly what she planned on doing.

"Well, it's certainly good to dream big." The officer laughed. "Were you here when the call was placed?"

"Yes. It was the neighbor's kid who just went to the park with his mother. They should be back shortly, if you want to wait and speak with them, maybe thirty minutes or so. Would you like to come in? I'm just about to make dinner."

The handsome cop considered his options. The female was so gorgeous, he almost wanted to take her up on her offer, but he was on the clock, and a home-cooked meal and pretty face just wasn't worth it. Besides, the call was bullshit. He'd done his job.

"No, but thank you for the offer. Nothing further is needed."

Honey closed the door and began to pace back and forth in her living room.

Luther didn't know the full extent of her worry, but he knew that cops coming to the door and a beat-up and possibly raped young white female couldn't lead to anything but heat coming down on everyone.

Honey thought quickly. She walked to the closet where Chief and the girl were still struggling. "Let go of her!" she commanded.

Once again the girl ran to Honey for protection.

"What has he done to you?"

Pumpkin didn't hesitate to drop dime. "He beat me and robbed me for all my money. Almost three hundred dollars of my hard-earned money!"

Honey glared at Chief. "So you tried to call the police, to help you, right?"

"Yes, but he stopped me." Pumpkin's tears began flowing once again as she relieved the horror.

"He's disgusting!" Honey said.

"Yo, you better watch your mouth, Honey!" Chief spat.

"I don't gotta do a muthafuckin' thing up in my house!" Honey cut her eyes at Chief and then refocused on the girl. "Don't worry. You're safe with me. Why don't you go and take a shower, and I'll bring you fresh clothes and make sure I get you your money back with interest."

A relieved Pumpkin said, "What about my things? My gun and cell phone?"

"I'll bring all that into the bathroom, but I will have to take the bullets out of your gun. I can't have you putting a bullet in my brother . . . although he deserves it."

Pumpkin was satisfied with her demands and retreated to the bathroom.

Once she was gone Honey stated, "You're gonna have to clean up your mess."

"I ain't got no money."

"You're as dumb as the day is long," Luther began. "You think Honey is talkin' 'bout you payin' off a whore?"

Chief resented that Luther and Honey thought he wasn't smart. "Then stop talkin' in riddles 'n' shit. I'm a direct type of dude. I keep it one hundred."

"Look, moron, you beat and robbed a prostitute, and God only knows what else. If we pay her off, in a few days she'll want to know why. And then she'll come around and want to get more money. What if she has a pimp? You brought this to my front door. I can't get knocked, and neither can you, not when we're in the middle of something this big. You want me to say it?" Honey hushed her voice. "She has to go."

Chief smiled at the realization. "You ain't said nothing but a word."

♠♠♠

Chief took pleasure in strangling the unsuspecting Pumpkin in the bathroom of his sister's apartment. Honey felt awful, but she didn't have a choice. Pumpkin knew the hazards of her occupation. The four-foot-eleven mother of four was stuffed into a black kitchen plastic bag, which was sat by the door to be dumped like trash. From there, Honey, Luther, and Chief scrubbed down the whole apartment wiping away any fingerprints and vacuuming any microscopic evidence that the naked eye couldn't see, such as strands of hair follicles or broken fingernails.

"Everyone needs to strip buttnaked and toss their clothes into a trash bag."

"I'm not tossing in my Tims," Chief complained. "You could forget that."

"Didn't you just rob this poor woman for three bills?"

Chief didn't even answer.

"Thought so."

Chief reluctantly decided to take off his Tims and toss them in the trash bag. After everyone had redressed, Honey then emptied all the contents of her vacuum cleaner into another bag and then tossed the remaining trash bags in it as well and then tied it shut, all the while handling each trash bag with gloves.

"Why did you throw away the rest of them good bags?" Luther asked and then answered his own question. "If five-O found these bags, they could trace them back to the remaining bags in your crib, correct?"

"No doubt. Each trash bag has an indexing system etched into them for each batch. If they happened to find the bag she's buried in and somehow connect her to this knucklehead and my apartment, it would only take a lab technician a few weeks to connect my trash bags to the scene of the crime. I've come too far to fuck up this early in the game."

"You ain't never lie when you said you learned so much from your ATF training. That training just saved your brother's ass!"

"Stop ridin' her shit. You act like she Einstein or some shit. Honey ain't never do nothing so great in her life. She out here starvin' just like I am. She ain't better than none of us. She ain't got a real job, and just commanded me to do a murder on a chick I wouldn't have ever thought to take out. So stop treating her like she some angel. And let's not go there on her marrying the same nigga that tried to dead me. But look what that same snake-ass muthafucka did to her ass!"

Honey laughed. Her brother was such a hater. He'd just overlooked the fact that she got him to do the dirty work and commit the murder on a woman he'd just said he would have let walk out the front door. So although he'd said she wasn't Einstein, she sure knew how to manipulate others and mastermind a crime. That had to count for something.

"Chief, we got too much to do than argue over the past. André is my past, and I've accepted and taken responsibility for all that's happened." I pulled off my gloves and redirected my attention toward my father. "Luther, you and Chief need to go and dump her in the desert, while I find a dumpster for our clothes. We can't dump them both in the same place. And, Chief?"

"Yes."

"Make sure you dig the grave deep enough that the coyotes and wolves can't pull her up."

Chapter 4

The stale, pungent odor was enough to jolt me awake after a restless night's sleep. I woke up to the horrible sight of my father's wrinkled penis just inches away from my face. He must have stumbled home drunk and passed out in my bed. He reeked of dried vomit and other bodily fluids that made me hold my nose in pure disgust. I took both hands and tried to shove him off my bed, but he was immovable, like deadweight. Eventually, I slapped his face several times trying to wake him up out of his drunken stupor, but I knew that was in vain.

"Get out of here!" I screamed, kicking my feet out like a small child having a tantrum. I was losing it. I was fed up over my living situation and the way my life had taken a sharp turn right into a brick wall.

Stumbling out of bed, I thought things couldn't get anymore horrifying, until I stepped into a glob of wet, slimy vomit. Apparently he'd tried to take a shower but had only made it halfway down the hall before his insides spewed up and he found the nearest bed to collapse in.

I spent the next hour mopping floors and washing my father and brother's clothing before I headed out to work. I had the three to eleven shift—the worst shift at the casino—but I was a newbie and work is work, no matter what time you clock in.

Nine hours later my father was still in a comatose-like sleep, and Chief wasn't anywhere to be found.

Ever since Big Meech and Delano had arrived, Chief had been

staying with them at the Super 8 Motel off S. Koval Lane. I worried because there was no policing their behavior from way over here at my apartment, but there wasn't any way I was allowing all three of them to temporarily live here. They'd do something asinine and send us all to jail.

Kicking off my lime green Manolo's and Bellagio uniform, I poured myself a glass of Sauvignon Blanc and began counting down the days to freedom from all the bullshit.

I heard rustling come from my room. I called out, "Daddy?"

"Yeah?"

"Could I have my bed back?" I said, my tone borderline hostile.

A couple minutes later, my father came out of my room wearing an ill-fitted pink bathrobe with his large feet protruding out of my bedroom slippers. That sight alone broke any tension or aggravation I had previously felt. *Leave it to Luther to be this ridiculous.*

We both erupted in a full-on belly laugh.

"I'm sorry about last night, Little Bit."

"It's all good, Daddy. I'm just under a lot of pressure lately, that's all. I don't mean to be bitchy."

"Sure, you did, but I still forgive you."

"Cool."

"Where's your brother?"

"Who knows? I just hope he keeps his ass out of trouble . . . at least for the next week."

"Hold that thought while I go get dressed."

"What thought?"

"Honey, when you gonna realize you can't run that jive game on your old man? You mentioned that Chief needed to stay clean for another week. You knew that wouldn't get past me, so let me get dressed, and let's go get a drink and you're gonna give me the four-one-one."

"But, Daddy, I don't wanna go back out," I whined.

"Too bad. I need a drink to get over my hangover."

My father took me to a seedy hole-in-the-wall bar. The type of joint that served liquor in white plastic cups, where almost everyone sitting at the bar was over fifty, contrasting with the stream of young women that just walked in.

A clan of ghetto chicks looking to find a sugar daddy was amusing to me. *Times could never get that hard for me*, I thought. "I shudder to think how you found this place."

"You know I make any town mines." Luther then signaled the bartender. "Pete, I'll take two Rémy's straight up and a club soda on the side."

The bartender nodded. "Sure thing, Luther."

"I'm sure you can see that this establishment don't make them fruity girly drinks."

"That's cool."

As we sipped on our drinks, not until I was sure we had complete privacy, did I begin to tell my father about my layered plans.

"We're going to knock off the Bellagio *and* Harrah's Casinos next Wednesday."

"Wow! That's a tall drink of water, Honey."

I nodded.

"I always did teach you to be ambitious."

"I wouldn't go that far," I joked.

"Since I'm coming in on the backend, I don't want to insult you by asking, have you done all the necessary intel on these two operations?"

"Everything is on point. I've worked on this for close to a year."

"To successfully pull this off, without it being just a really good failed attempt, it would take just that long."

I took in his words. "Well, truthfully, the hardest part was finding my crew. I needed to profile everyone to make sure they had what it took and wouldn't buckle under pressure. One weak link and the whole chain collapses."

"The Bellagio and Harrah's," Luther repeated. "I can honestly say I'm nervous for you, Little Bit. No one has successfully robbed those casinos, Honey. The security alone is tighter than a virgin's pussy. Shit, the Secret Service might as well be guarding those casinos. It's risky—"

"But not impossible."

"Well, nothing is impossible if you have strong will."

"Which I have. But being strong-willed isn't enough. I need to align all the perfect storms in order at the perfect time, and if I have all those things, then I'll walk away with millions."

"And you're working on that?"

"Exactly."

"I figured you for a lot of things—a hustler's wife, an honor student, the daughter of an ex-con, an ATF agent, a mother, sister, grandmother⊠ but I never figured you could do this level of a crime. I guess what I'm saying is, you could be anything you put your mind toward. Why this?"

"I got a few scores to settle, a few creditors to pay back, so I thought, why the hell not?"

"Nah, I'm being serious. You're taking a big chance here."

I didn't want to get serious. Not the serious he was looking for. I was in too deep, and I wanted him to be my co-pilot. Right now he was being Negative Nelly, and I wasn't feeling it. My reasons are my reasons. Him trying to psychoanalyze me in a seedy bar on a back alley was irritating.

"You sound surprised. I got Luther Brown blood flowing through my veins. I got your smarts and your penchant for illegal gains. It is what it is. I grew up around crime all my life. Something had to rub off on me."

"But, Honey—"

"Luther, you always told me, without risk there's no reward. I'm telling you I was built to do this. You have to have faith in me. I need you right now."

"OK, run it down to me and don't leave out any details. Pete, another round!"

♠♠♠

"Bitch, what the fuck you looking at?"

My eyes focused on a dark-skinned girl perched on the barstool. She had bleach-blonde hair, hazel contacts, and her ghetto diamonds on. Apparently she was the ringleader of her crew of three she was sitting with.

"I'm not looking at you. I'm looking past you." I rose up. I was actually looking at a familiar face, the girls from Neiman Marcus and the casinos. "But we could get it on and poppin' and take this outside."

"Oh, you don't want to take this outside because, I promise you, if I get up, I'll slaughter your silly ass. I'm nice wit' mines."

In one swift movement, I grabbed the chick up out of her seat and body-slammed her on the dirty wooden floor. Her lace-front wig dangled in my hands as I began stomping her guts out with my six-inch stilettos.

"One of y'all bitches jump in this fight and touch my daughter, and I'll put a donut hole in ya head!" Luther flashed his pistol, and the other three women backed off.

I whipped on the bigmouth mercilessly until the bartender Pete click-clacked his shotgun. That sound alone was intimidating. Pete called his bouncers to throw out the wolf pack, and Luther and I resumed where we left off.

"Damn, girl! You still got it."

I didn't respond to Luther because I was too heated and still in war mode. "How's my face?" I asked, breathing heavily.

"Your face?" Luther replied. "You should be concerned about your knuckles."

I could feel a stinging coming from the back of my neck. I passed my hand back there and then looked at it and was relieved when I didn't see any blood.

"I'll be right back," I said to Luther. I grabbed my bag and walked off to the bathroom, where I pulled out my small mirror, and with the mirror that was already on the bathroom wall, I was able to examine the back of my neck, where I saw a huge welt, but there was no blood.

I would've exchanged getting scratched on the back of my neck for dishing out a beatdown any day of the week. So after confirming that I had only been scratched, I felt better and returned to where Luther was sitting.

"Listen, Pete, I'm sorry about that little altercation," I said to him.

"It's all good. Actually, I think that bitch who got her ass beat is more sorry than you are right now." Pete laughed and gave Luther a pound.

"They come in here a lot?" I asked.

Pete curled up his bottom lip as he thought for a moment. "Actually, no, they don't. I don't really remember ever seeing them before. I might have seen the bleach-blonde once or twice before."

I nodded my head to him, and then Luther reminded me again that I still had my hand game intact.

"At least for another ten years," I bragged. "I'm only twenty-five. She couldn't fuck with me in my sleep."

"You get your hand game from my side of the family. Back in my day, your aunts use to terrorize a whole neighborhood."

I chuckled because I had grown up hearing the stories. "And where did you get that pistol?"

"Oh, this here?" Luther patted his waist. "This belong to that young girl Chief had to dispose of. Couldn't let a good thing like this go to waste."

"You know what I'm about to say before I even say it."

"That this gun could either be dirty, or registered to a murdered girl. Either way, I'm a dumb muthafucka for carrying it."

I looked past Luther. "Daddy, give me a minute, OK."

I walked over to the two women that I'd been consistently seeing. I wasn't sure why, but my sixth sense told me to. "Excuse me."

They both looked up.

"My name is Honey, and I've been seeing you two around a lot."

"Yeah, we've been seeing you too. Real recognize real. We loved your work in Neiman Marcus."

I smiled.

"This is Blythe, and my name is Tee-Tee. We put in work too."

"Is that so?"

"Yeah, we do all types of get-money schemes to make a living," Blythe said.

"We was about to jump in and kick some ass, had any of those bum-ass bitches tried to jump you," Tee-Tee added. "But we saw you and your father had that under control."

"Oh, no doubt. But good looking-out. Hey, why don't I get y'all numbers? I might have something that could be a quick come-up. I don't have all the particulars, but I'll fill y'all in once I know for sure."

The women both gave me their contacts, and with that, Luther and I left. It was late, and I was exhausted from the beatdown, which sucked all the energy right out of me.

Chapter 5

I adjusted my stiff neck from side to side, and ran my right hand across the blackjack table before pulling each card from the Shuffle Master dispenser one by one. I had a packed table of six players hell-bent on bankrupting the house. All the players looked at their hands, just barely peering at their cards. They were definitely pros. One player hit the table, a sign he wanted another card. He then gestured his hand toward the right, which meant he was staying with the hand he was dealt. I topped off each player with additional cards until they were satisfied with their hands. All of the players decided to stand, which was a good move because everyone was showing a seventeen and better. And as the dealer, I was showing a six, which meant I had to take a hit and there was a good chance that I would bust and everybody would win.

"No. Wait. You know what? I changed my mind. Hit me, sweetie," an old lady sitting at the end of the table said to me, her voice cracking from old age. She was chain-smoking cigarettes and downing shots of liquor and her wrinkled skin told me that she was close to eighty years old and probably blowing her Social Security check at my table.

"Ma'am, are you sure?" I asked.

"Granny, what the hell are you doing?" a young muscle-bound Italian dude said to the old lady. "You're showing an eight."

"I'm not your granny! Sonny boy, if you call me that again I'll pop you good!" the feisty old white lady yelled. She smacked the palm of her right hand on the table and demanded that I hit her with another card.

I was trying my hardest not to laugh, trying to keep it professional, and managed to hold it together. I pulled another card from the deck and laid it down in front of the old lady. "Ten!" I yelled and quickly scooped up the old lady's chips because she had just bust with a twenty-eight.

I turned over my card that wasn't exposed, and it was a Queen, which meant that I now had a sixteen. Had the old lady not taken that hit, her Ten would have been my Ten, and as the dealer, I would have bust and everyone at the table would have won.

I pulled the next card from the deck to hit my hand, and low and behold, it was a Five. "Twenty-one," I shouted.

I did a clean sweep and picked up all the players' cards and then chips. The old lady didn't seem like she too much cared, because she had only wagered twenty-five dollars on that hand. As for all of the other players, all that cash just went to the house. At least eight thousand dollars.

I thought about one player who'd just lost five of the eight grand. Imagine what a whole family could do with five thousand dollars. And he certainly had a family, at least a wife. His shiny gold band said so. I'd been watching people lose and lose some more for the past year. Sometimes they just hung their heads and headed home. Others drowned their misery in the bar, only to come back hours later and try again.

"Muthafucka!" the young Italian dude yelled out after realizing that he'd lost all of his money, thanks to the old lady.

One of the other frustrated players at the table said, "This old bitch has to be working for the casino."

I chuckled and shook my head no.

Another player said, "Granny, can you please step aside and give your seat to someone else?"

"I'm not your goddamn granny! My money is just as good as yours, and if you're so afraid of losing your money, then what are you doing here? This is a casino. Haven't you ever heard that scared money don't make money?" the old lady said emphatically. She reached into her pocketbook and pulled out two hundred and fifty dollars in chips and placed them in front of her to let me know that she was ready for more action.

I let out a little bit of laughter. I couldn't help it.

"Oh, and you think it's funny, Honey?" the muscle-bound dude asked me, after reading my name tag.

"I'm so sorry," I said to all of the players. But they were way too frustrated to play another hand with the old lady, and they all got up and went to find another table to play at.

Just at that moment I spotted my brother from way across the room. He'd just come in, with Big Meech and Delano trailing not far behind. Cinnamon was holding Meech's arm tight, and I could see everyone was scanning the room. When our eyes locked, I could see Chief was about to do exactly what I told him not to. Seconds later the whole crew bought in at my table and began playing alongside Granny.

I was grooming a bunch of imbeciles. I guess the warning "Don't come to my table while I'm on duty" didn't register with any of them.

Soon the old lady's luck did a one eighty, and she began playing her hot streak until she was ready to tap out. She stood up and announced, "This beautiful young lady will take good care of you." She began collecting her chips. "I just killed 'em for five hundred dollars." Granny then tossed me a twenty-five-dollar chip as a tip. She gave me a wink. "That's for you. Buy yourself something nice."

"Thank you, ma'am," I said.

She leaned in and said to me, "My strategy works every time. I always win right after flushing out all the pussies."

"Woaaaow!" I laughed.

Granny was the quintessential old-school gambler with an addiction. I was sure she was a regular at most casinos. Unfortunately, I couldn't give her anymore of my time or attention because I had Chief and his boys to attend to.

At first, no one said a thing. They just all played along like we were strangers.

When Granny finally moved on, Chief said, "Yo, you better start doin' something with those cards, so we can all eat."

I smirked.

"It's hotter than Satan's balls, in a casino. Don't you know that we're constantly watched by the cameras?" Before Chief could move, I added. "And don't look up, dummy. If you do, I promise you that Bradley, our head of security, will peep that and have five goons from the back follow you out to your car, take your license plate number, and God only knows what else."

"I wish a nigga would try to raise up on me!" Chief began to get animated. "These my eyes. They can't stop me from looking."

Big Meech began looking around nervously. "Chief, man, lower your voice. You makin' us hot."

"That's all, Honey," Chief said defiantly. "All she had to do was hit us off with twenty-one so we could have some club money to blow, but even that was too much. If she ain't the one giving orders, she ain't down. All she care about is herself."

"You are more girl than me." I was aggravated. "It's never easy with you, is it?" Although I knew better, I stopped shuffling the deck to argue with Chief over bullshit.

"Honey, is everything all right?" Alonzo, my immediate supervisor, asked, the faint sound of a walkie-talkie in the distance.

I looked up to see Bradley glaring at the table, ready to pounce if I gave him the word. "Yeah, everything is OK. These gentlemen were just asking what they could get into while in Vegas. They wanted to see the sights. I told them I only know blackjack."

Sternly, Alonzo said, "Either play or keep it moving. This ain't no travel agency."

You could see agitation written on everyone's face. They all wanted to scream on Alonzo but fortunately thought wisely.

"Yo, money, since you the boss and shit, why don't you get one of them fine cocktail shorties over here to hit us off with some of them free drinks they passing out?" Big Meech said. "Chief, what a nigga want?"

"Oh yeah. I forgot drinks is free up in this bitch. Get me some of that VSOP on the rocks," Chief replied.

"Word! Yo make that two of those, and bring us two Bacardi and Coke on the rocks," Big Meech said to Alonzo.

Alonzo looked like he wanted to flip the fuck out, but he remained calm and composed. "You're just going to have to play, and the waitresses will make their way over to you eventually," Alonzo said.

"Eventually?" Big Meech asked. "What does that mean? We thirsty now! Ain't you a shot-caller? A pit boss or something like that? Get on that Secret Service mic that y'all got and get niggas some drinks."

Thankfully Big Meech went into his pocket and pulled out two hundred dollars, and I was able to give him some chips so that he looked like a real blackjack player and not just a black ghetto buffoon. Alonzo backed off, and we were able to play about four hands.

The cocktail waitress eventually did make it to my table, and she gave Chief and everyone drinks that she already had on her tray.

"Yeah, this what the fuck I'm talkin' about," Big Meech said as he took two drinks from the tray.

Chief took a drink and then started flirting with the cocktail waitress. "Ma, where you from? Venezuela or something like that? You just look all good, and tropical and shit."

The waitress smiled and shook her head. "I'm from New Jersey."

"Word? Brick City? You ain't from Newark, are you?"

She shook her head no.

"But I'm saying, where are your parents from? Because all that thick tropicalness you got going on, they don't grow that out in Jersey."

"My parents are from Peru. I'm Peruvian," the waitress replied. She was obviously waiting for a tip, but it was a tip that never came.

I was thoroughly embarrassed and pissed off all at the same time, and I wanted them all to just leave.

Chief must have been able to read my mind, because he was preparing to get up and leave the table. Just as he was getting up, he said, "Yo, y'all heard about Dré? He got married last week to Olivia from a hundred and thirty-fifth. Yo, that chick is bad as hell."

My stomach dropped at the mere mention of my ex and the same chick I'd busted him eating out, but I couldn't give Chief the satisfaction of a reaction.

Within seconds, everyone scattered and a new batch of players began to fill in the empty seats.

"Next time you got a table full of wise guys, you alert somebody. I spot losers like that a mile away." Alonzo ran his hand slowly down the crease of my back. A little too slowly. "In fact, when you get off, come and find me so I can walk you to your car. You can never be too careful. One of those punks could be lying in wait for you."

I smiled appreciatively. "Oh, thank you. But I'm meeting a friend tonight when I get off, so I'll be fine."

Alonzo seemed like he wanted to press the issue but knew his behavior was bordering on sexual harassment. "OK, that's good. Later."

"Bye." I looked back up to see Bradley was still there watching.

♠♠♠

I wouldn't say I had a hard day at work, but my interest was surely piqued. Why had Bradley lingered? That one little gesture, however small, was enough to have my mind racing. I didn't want to overthink the situation, because that's when you mess up. But I couldn't afford to overlook the smallest detail. With the heist only days away, my mind had to perform at its full potential, which was hard to do, with Chief and his nursery of knuckleheads providing me with distraction after distraction.

My telephone began to vibrate just as I walked into the ladies' room to change my clothes. He was right on time.

"Hey, baby."

"I'll be out in five minutes. I'm just changing out of this stuffy uniform. Are you out front?"

"Yeah, I'm out front. About six cars from the entrance. You'll see me."

"Just make sure no one else does," I warned.

"I'm straight."

"OK, five minutes."

"Take your time. We got all night," he said, and blew a kiss through the phone.

♠♠♠

The pale-green colored, skintight cold-shoulder dress by the Kardashian sisters' new line, Dash, looked painted on. The raw silk material hugged my every curve. Being five feet tall, I couldn't be caught dead in less than six-inch heels. The green and yellowish-gold color heels accented my smooth, honey-brown complexion. I think I came out my mother's womb in stilettos. I had a shoe fetish that kept my bank account on zero.

As I pranced through the hotel making my way to the exit, I saw a flurry of events—a Detroit pimp in a white fur hat, pinstripe suit, and red gators working the floor with his three prostitutes; at least two professional jostlers that I was aware of (God only knows how many more were littered through each casino); a stable of athletes, from NBA to NFL, throwing large sums of money on not only the games but the women as well.

What I didn't like seeing was Natasha engrossed at the roulette table and looking like she'd been there all night. Her clothes looked disheveled and in disarray, and you could see the dark circles under her eyes from a mile away. Her brittle, bleach-blonde hair looked dirty and lifeless. Her body language was that of someone who was defeated but refused to be beaten. Her shoulders hunched over, her eyes were intently focused on the game. She was truly an addict and hadn't taken my warning seriously at all. I made a note to myself to speak with her once again about getting help. At the rate she was going, she was going to blow all her heist money right back at the very casino she ripped off.

Las Vegas is certainly a city that never sleeps. New York has nothing on this little town. Sin City, I thought.

I exited the entrance to my left and immediately spotted Brian, who was hunched down low in his dark blue Ford Mustang, a blue, fitted NY Yankees cap on his head. When he saw me, he rose up, slightly.

As I approached the vehicle I heard, "Honey."

We both looked. Mercedes was steadily approaching.

I hopped in the passenger seat, but she was already at Brian's window, tapping. He kept his face toward me while rolling down the window.

"Where are you off too so fast?" she asked, straining her neck to get a good look at Brian.

"I'm sorry, miss, but you must have me confused with someone else," I said.

Mercedes looked perplexedly and then caught on. "Oh yeah, you're right. I thought you were my friend. You looked so much like her from a distance." She began to back away. "I'm sorry I bothered you."

"No bother at all."

Brian rolled up the window and then slowly peeled out. "Wow!

That shit was close," he said.

"You telling me? Do you think she got a good look at you?" I asked, worried.

"Nah, not at all."

"You sure?"

"Look, stop worrying."

I sat back. "OK, if you say so."

Brian and I went to a Thai restaurant on the other side of town where no one knew us and we were free to be ourselves. We could kiss, snuggle, laugh, flirt and not worry about looking over our shoulders.

"I know cheap men across the world are so happy for Thai restaurants," I said, teasing him. "You can get good, quality food for under ten bucks."

"Come on, Honey. You know I ain't hardly cheap."

"That's exactly what you are."

"You know I'd be able to give you more but—"

"But you're too busy tricking on your wife and four kids."

"My soon-to-be ex-wife."

"That still lives under your roof."

"See, I told you that's only temporary until she can find a place of her own that she can afford. Right now we're only roommates dividing the expenses down the middle. She's leaving, and I get to keep the kids with me."

I looked at Brian. He had the most innocent eyes any woman could ever gaze upon.

"Why every time we're alone, talk turns into your wife and kids?"

"You're the one who keeps bringing them up. I'm happy just to be here with you eating my inexpensive Thai food, and hopefully you later."

"Just make sure you leave room for the dessert. I don't want you falling asleep in the pussy like you did last time."

Brian shook his head emphatically. "Why do you speak like that? And don't tell me it's because you're from the hood in New York, because so am I."

Immediately, I got angry. "Look, take this how it is. I'm a full package. You can't chip away at what you don't like and think you're going to remix my personality. At least I'm not sitting up here trying to be someone I'm not, like you are."

"How am I trying to be someone I'm not?"

"Right now you're trying to be *not* married." I cocked my head to one side. "How 'bout that?"

Brian exhaled. He had such patience and knew how to un-press the buttons he'd just pushed. "Look, gorgeous, I don't want to do this." He clasped his massive hands together.

Brian was a fairly large man with a square jawbone, outlined by a goatee. His thick eyebrows were smooth and framed his expressive eyes. His soft hair was always cut low, and his dark-chocolate skin was newborn-baby soft.

I knew his wife wasn't letting him go, and all that shit he was talking was just noise. "Can we just have a good night, just you and me, enjoying each other's company?"

"What time do you gotta be home?"

He fidgeted. "At least by six." He held up his hand. "Just in time to get the kids up and ready for school. That's the only reason. Had this been a weekend, you would have had me for the whole night."

"Good. So I'll fuck your brains out until five fifty-nine."

He kissed my lips.

"That works for me."

Funny, my vulgar mouth was no longer an issue.

When we left the restaurant, Brian wanted us to go to a hotel in Old Las Vegas, where the off-strip low-end hotels and casinos are located.

It's basically where all of the lowlife vagrants and winos hangout.

"Brian, take my ass home please."

"Babe, come on. I thought you was saying you'll fuck my brains out until five fifty-nine."

"Yes, and I will. But I'm not doing Old Las Vegas. I'm tired of that cheap shit. Now if you want to bring me to a high-end hotel on the strip, then by all means, this pussy is yours. But if not, then you know where I live."

Brian shook his head as he turned the car around and headed in the direction toward my house. There was dead silence in the car, that tight-mouthed silence that men exhibit when they can't get no pussy as promised. But I didn't give a fuck. I mean, I liked Brian and all, but at the same time, I had to make sure that I was respecting myself. I wasn't no cheap-trick whore from the strip that he could take to some seedy hotel whenever he wanted to fuck on moldy-ass, bedbug-infested mattresses. And there was definitely no way in hell I was going to fuck Brian in his car like some teenager on my high-school prom.

"Would you take your wife to Old Las Vegas?"

"In a heartbeat," Brian shot back, trying to be all quick-witted.

"Well, I ain't your wife! Tap her ass on the shoulder when you get in, and drive her back to Old Las Vegas and get your rocks off."

"Honey, what the hell happened, and what did I miss?"

I didn't answer him. While he drove, I decided to shoot a text to Stephon. *Hey* was all my text to him said.

What's up babe? I was just thinking about you.

I smiled when I saw his text. I responded, *Where are you?*

Stephon responded that he was driving and on his way to Los Angeles, that he would be back in Vegas the next afternoon around five.

Oh OK. I was just saying what's up. Drive safe. NO TEXTING AND DRIVING. Call me tomorrow. Love you.

"Who you texting this time of night?" Brian asked me.

I was no dummy. I needed Brian, and I knew exactly what I needed him for.

"I'm texting my brother, trying to see where he's at. I did promise you some, so we can do it at my crib, but I don't want us walking into no dysfunction," I explained.

I could feel Brian's entire mood shift. For the life of me I could never understand why men are so motivated by sticking their dick in some pussy. I'm sure the shit feels good to them, but it's like they give women puppet master control over them just because of it.

When we made it to my house, Chief wasn't home, and neither was Luther. I was so glad. I didn't know where Chief was at, but I was sure that Luther was down at the bar chasing skirts. Regardless, I didn't want them to meet or even see Brian because I was purposely not trying to mix business with pleasure and, in the process, jeopardize my ultimate goal.

"About that 'fucking until five fifty-nine' thing, yeah, I'm going to have to give you a rain check on that one because I don't want my father and brother coming home and totally blowing up my spot."

"It's all good." Brian immediately started kissing me as soon as we walked in the front door.

I could feel his dick poking through his pants. "I see somebody is super-excited," I said to him and then I led him into my bedroom.

With Brian I made sure that we always used a condom. With Stephon, the dick was so much better that it got to the point where we were always fucking without condoms. And I truly cared for him. But with Brian, I wasn't feeling him like that. He was my booty call with a purpose. I fucked him like it was part of my job description. I was never really all that into it, but I always faked it like he was slinging dick around like King Kong.

"I know how you like it," I said to him, smiling while undressing.

Brian took his pants off but left his shirt on. As he slipped a condom over his dick, I positioned myself on the bed with my face in the mattress and my ass up in the air.

"Face down, ass up. Right, baby?"

Before Brian could even answer me, he had slipped his dick into my pussy and was fucking me like an inexperienced sixteen-year-old. His rhythm and his strokes were all off, and he wasn't fucking me deep enough. But there was no way I was going to coach him through anything. I just did my best to fantasize about another man, which helped my pussy to stay wet so I could make it through the session. Thankfully, Brian wasn't a long-winded brother, and before too long, he was ready to cum and pulling his dick out and nutting all over my ass.

Every time Brian fucked me he would splash so much cum on me that I knew for sure he wasn't fucking at home on a regular basis. It always seemed like I was draining at least a week's worth of cum out of him.

"We really have to do the all-night thing," I said to him, in an attempt to boost his ego.

"We will. I promise. Just give me some time to work on shit at home," Brian explained as he put on his pants and prepared to leave.

I nodded my head and softly said, "OK." Then I kissed him on his lips before he departed.

Chapter 6

O K, let's go over the plan one more time," I said to a hushed crowd of five. We were less than a week away from the heist, and these last days were important. "A heist consists of three parts—the plan, the execution, and the getaway. If for any reason one of these elements aren't met, then we will be unsuccessful. It's that simple.

"Cinnamon, at approximately 7:16 a.m., Garda armored truck will pull up to Harrah's Casino and Hotel's back entrance on the strip. Two armed armored-car security guards will unload seventeen million dollars worth of casino chips."

"But, again, I know I keep asking this same question," Delano said. "What a nigga gonna do with chips?"

I exhaled. Delano had such a thick skull. Going over the plan with all this testosterone was certainly more challenging than when dealing with the ladies. The women listened and took directions easily. With this crew, everything was a struggle.

"The chips are plastic currency, Delano. I keep telling you that. The best thing about a con is that the mark doesn't know they are being conned. These chips are hiding in plain sight. Think about it," I said, getting animated, using my hands to make my point. "How many millions of dollars are right in front of you as you play blackjack or roulette? And not one person ever thinks about snatching the pot. Do you know why? Because it's disguised as something worthless. Put mud over a million-dollar diamond, and no one will see its worth. You feel me?"

"I feel you, Honey," Big Meech stated. "We hit the tables, and they won't know what's coming. All the heat will be protecting the backrooms and the cashiers. Those punk-ass dealers ain't gonna risk their lives over no chips. It'll take a matter of seconds to load up and walk out that front door carrying millions."

I smiled. At least one person was on the same page as I was.

"But that sound all good, Honey, when you say millions, but what if when Meech, Delano, and Chief go in and all they bring back are hundreds of dollar chips. Then what, huh?" Cinnamon liked her question. She'd thought long and hard before speaking, hoping to get everyone's attention and finally be treated as an equal. She was tired of being overlooked because of her age. She had just turned eighteen, but everyone treated her like she was twelve.

"Why are we even letting this moron be down with our fuckin' operation?" Big Meech barked.

Big Meech was a large, husky individual with massive biceps and triceps, a dead giveaway of the years he'd spent in Folsom State Prison bench-pressing heavy weights for recreation. At thirty-one, he'd already spent half his life in and out of correctional facilities on both the East Coast and the West. He'd settled down in New York eighteen months back when he followed his right-hand man Malik to do a home invasion. His man was killed on site, and he'd gotten away. He'd only planned to stay long enough to exact revenge for his slain homey, but the flashy city-never-sleeps lifestyle and sexy women kept his interest.

"I already told you why she's needed, and it's not for her brains. We need someone who can handle a car and also look inconspicuous sitting parked behind the stolen FedEx minivan."

After Cinnamon had given birth to Big Meech's daughter eight weeks earlier, things started going downhill from there between them. She was hoping that they'd actually pull off this heist because, with the money, she planned that her and Big Meech would get far away from Vegas and even farther away from Chief and Delano and their ghetto ways. Cinnamon felt that they were a bad influence on him and the separation would do their relationship some good. When she found out that Honey had sent money for them to come down to Vegas, she demanded she be allowed to come too. She'd even paid her way on the Greyhound bus and left their daughter with her mother.

"Honey, the chips are plastic currency, and they aren't traceable, like you said. But the thing you have to remember is, each casino has its own chips," Delano said.

"Don't you think I know that?" I replied.

"Nah, what I'm getting at is, how the fuck will we cash these chips in? After we hit, Harrah's Casino will be hot as hell. We'll have to sit on them chips for a minute before we cash them in."

Delano was making good points, but he was acting as if I hadn't thought this shit through. His overthinking was interfering with my master plan. I didn't bring him in to think. I brought him in to follow orders, which Chief told me his crew would do.

Delano continued, "Honey, all I'm saying is that, let's say hundred-dollar chips are black and white. What's to stop the casino from changing the color of hundred-dollar chips and then putting an expiration date on the black-and-white hundred-dollar chips just to flush out the person who's sitting on the stolen chips?"

"Delano, listen, I got this, OK. It's already taken care of, and that's already been considered. We're good," I replied. "Trust me. They can't and won't put an expiration date on the chips. I've read the casino bylaws from the Gaming Commission thoroughly, and we're good. Now can we get back to business?"

"I told y'all my sister was book-smart," Chief bragged. "Now, if anyone of y'all muthafuckas read the casino bylaws, raise your hand. If not, shut the fuck up and let her finish."

No one said a word, so I continued.

"Big Meech, you and Chief will already be in the cut inside the casino. Meech, you'll be at the high rollers table playing baccarat. Chief, you'll be at the roulette table. Those tables hold the most chips, at least a million dollars each. Delano will be the lookout for when the guards begin to change shifts. That's at approximately 7:53a.m.

"When you see Javier, head of security, talk into his wrist, that means he's just told all his underlings that the floor is secure and that they can make their way to the back. The moment he puts his arm to his waist, you put your Uzi in his spine and tell him not to make a muthafuckin' move or he's dead."

"I can handle that," Delano said reassuringly.

"I know you can," I encouraged. "Next, you get on your walkie-talkie and say, 'Set it off!'"

"And that's when I can get busy." Chief jumped up with two pistols, one in each hand. "I'ma say, 'Nobody move! Nobody gets hurt!'"

Big Meech laughed. "That's my nigga. While you and Delano are covering me and holding down the floor, I'm loading up our knapsacks with the chips."

"I feel that we should have some type of explosive or some shit. To really set that muthafucka off." Chief looked in full contemplation.

"Explosives?"

"Yeah, something like a grenade to toss while we're making our exit."

"This ain't the movies, Chief," I told him. "You wanna blow all y'all asses up? You've never been trained on using explosives, have you?"

"Ain't nobody train my ass to let my gat go, but a nigga do it, right? There you go thinking you a muthafuckin' Einstein. I done told you about that shit, Honey."

"OK, be easy now, Chief," Luther replied. "Ain't no need for you to keep taking shit so personally."

"Luther, you not gonna keep going against me just 'cause she your blood."

"Like hell, I will!" Luther stood up and towered over the five-foot-six Chief.

Chief would never admit it, but Luther intimated the hell out of him. He always did. "Honey don't even like your drunk ass!"

"Enough! We're here to get that money, and all this bickering shit isn't necessary. You're worse than a room full of bitches. We all need each other, or else this plan won't work. Chief, negative on the explosives, OK."

"I was just trying to enhance the plan, that's all."

"And it's appreciated, but we got lots to get through today." I refocused my attention on my father. "Luther, you'll be on the outside listening to the police scanner to see how far five-O is. There's a four-minute response time from when the call or alarm is initiated to point of arrival. You'll be in charge of keeping the guys on schedule. They have exactly two minutes from when Delano gives them the signal and make it out the front door, where Cinnamon will be waiting. You'll also tail behind them in a throwaway car, keeping your distance, just in case the heat gets on them. You'll be a distraction to hinder and run interference. Any coppers get too close, throw on your emergency brake and spin out."

"Now that might be a little too risky," Luther objected.

"If the heat is on our asses, you better do something!" Chief yelled. "If everyone doesn't do their part, when it comes time to break bread, muthafuckas ain't getting paid. Family or not, I can promise you that."

"Word!" Big Meech agreed. "We going buck wild up in that piece, and the only thing you're expected to do is have a little fender-bender?

Get the fuck outta here! And you beefin'? Yet you gonna eat what we eat?"

"Look, I'm an old man. My body can't take too many bumps and bruises," Luther explained.

"If you can't take the heat, get out the kitchen," Cinnamon stated.

"Shut the fuck up! Would you do us all that favor?" Big Meech snapped.

"No! You shut the fuck up!" Cinnamon said, finding her voice. "You, you, you, big bully!"

Big Meech took his massive hand and, with one slap, leveled Cinnamon. Her head hit the floor so hard, I thought he'd split it open. Everyone gasped at the sound. Seconds later, however, Cinnamon was back on her feet, scratching and clawing at her baby daddy. We all intervened, and the meeting came to an abrupt end, while I stayed back to console the injured Cinnamon.

"Why do you allow him to put his hands on you? You're better than that."

"I didn't," she said, her face stained with tears and grief. "You see I fought him back."

"You *tried* to fight him back. Your little baby punches could hardly penetrate someone as big and muscular as Big Meech. I'm talking about leaving him."

"And go where? With what? My looks?" She snorted disgust at her own dire situation. "And what about our baby?"

"Well, after we pull off the Harrah's job, you'll have your own money to do what you please. You mean to tell me that you'd still stay with him and subject your baby to the dysfunction?"

"That money won't be mines. I thought I'd be able to get the money and leave him." She wiped her tearstained face with the back of her hand. "He's already said that he's taking my cut."

"Taking your cut? How you figure?"

"Honey, once we split the money, who's going to stop him from taking my money?"

I thought for a moment. My brain was already remixing the plan, which was something I tried to shy away from. It was too risky.

"Let me ask you a question, and I want you to answer honestly. If you could choose between having your own money or living life out with your baby daddy, which would you choose?"

Cinnamon lowered her eyes.

"And you can't have both. So what would your choice be?"

"I'd choose the money. I hate to admit that, but I would choose the money."

I nodded. "Good answer."

Chapter 7

When I walked into the back room of Party's mother's house, the playful mood shifted. The joking around stopped. I stared at Natasha and could visibly see her discomfort.

She shifted in her seat and adjusted her collar around her neck. Sweat began to form under the pits of her arms, omitting a slight odor, which began to permeate the room.

"So what happened last night?"

"Honey, you know how it is."

"Actually, I don't."

"Ummm, well, the last time you and I spoke—"

"Natasha, don't fuckin' recap what I already know. Tell me what I don't."

"OK, OK, I just didn't do it, OK. Are you happy? I fucked up. I was supposed to leave Monday and go to Arizona to lift our getaway car for the heist, but I got caught up in the casino. I was playing my hot streak, Honey. You gotta feel me on that."

"You were playing a hot streak worth what? One stack? Two? When we're about to pull off the biggest heist in Las Vegas history? Are you a fuckin' idiot?"

"If I'm an idiot, then what are you? You're the one who pulled me in knowing I had an addiction. You're supposed to be the fuckin' mastermind or something, so you should have seen this coming a mile away." Natasha laughed, and she began to relax. She continued, growing confident in her words, "It's just a little hiccup. Like what the fuck? You actin' like I killed somebody. It's only a car. I can grab a car anywhere, and we're still good."

Mercedes said, "Don't you think Honey had already considered us grabbing a car from anywhere? There was a reason you were supposed to snatch the car out of state. Do you think you're the only one in here to have a plan B?"

"Nobody's even talking to you."

"Well, I'm talking to you."

I never took my gaze off Natasha. I always knew she was a wildcard, but she was good at what she did, so I took my chances and gambled. I didn't lose, though, because I was still playing a winning hand.

"Y'all so hypnotized. Honey got all y'all shook. But I ain't scared of no fuckin' body! And if anyone in here even thinks about cutting me out of the deal, I'll go to the fuckin' feds! I swear on everything I love, I'll do it! Y'all think you're going to divide up all that cash without me? Well, you better think again."

"Nobody's going to divide up the cash without you, Natasha," I said, "because you don't exist."

Party stepped forward with a garrote in her hand.

Natasha's eyes widened from sheer panic and fear. She lunged forward, in an effort to knock Party over, but Party grabbed a hold of her collar, and they both fell over the coffee table, which ended up in splinters.

From there, it was pound for pound. Party would hit, and Natasha would throw a punch back. Not only was Natasha outpunched, but she was outsized. Party began tossing her around like a rag doll as we all watched in amusement. Natasha was more formidable than I'd ever imagined. Her lean body frame could actually withstand severe trauma.

Soon a knife entered the fray. The plan was for Party to strangle Natasha to death. Simple. Clean. Party lifted the eleven-inch blade, something a person would use to carve a turkey, high above her head and then shoved it in Natasha's back.

Natasha let out a low moan as her knees buckled.

Just as Party was about to thrust the knife once again, I commanded, "Stop!"

No one moved. It was like I had pushed a "pause" button.

Natasha took my words as a sign of weakness. "Honey, don't let her do this. I'm not dead yet. This can all be fixed. Just drop me off to a hospital, and I swear, I won't tell the police shit. I was just fuckin' around."

I tossed Party the duct tape. "Silence that bitch!"

"Honey, no-o-o-o!"

Natasha screamed until Party almost had her face gift-wrapped. She tried to fight back, but it was a weak attempt. She was losing pints of blood by the minute.

At that moment I realized I was good at ad-libbing. I grabbed a heavy-duty plastic bag. "Tie up her hands and feet and toss her in the bag. She's leaving a bloody mess, which is evidence."

"I'm sorry, Honey," Party said.

"It's all good."

Party said, "Mercedes, help me tape up her hands and feet."

Mercedes walked over to assist Party to subdue the still defiant Natasha.

"Wait!" I said to Mercedes. "Put on gloves when handling that tape. I don't expect authorities to ever find her body, but if they do, they'd have a field day pulling your prints off that sticky tape."

Mercedes exhaled. "Thanks, bossy. Always one step ahead."

After we'd successfully gotten Natasha in the plastic bag, I ordered Party to put a plastic bag over her face and put her out of her misery. From there we cleaned up all the blood from off the floor, washed it down with bleach. Was that foolproof? Not at all. If a forensic team had come in here with luminol, it would have still picked up traces of her DNA. But the thorough cleanup ensured that they would have never even considered looking in here for any forensic evidence.

The heist was less than twenty-four hours away, and we were on our way to the Nevada desert to drop a body in a pre-dug grave. Party and Mercedes rode in the dirty car, while myself, Tee-Tee, and Blythe followed shotgun, with Tee-Tee at the wheel.

"So what now, Honey?"

"What's up?" I asked, clearly in another world.

"Like, what are we going to do now? We're one girl down, and we don't have the getaway vehicle."

"Have you ever heard the expression 'one monkey don't stop no show'?" Not waiting for a response, I added, "There's always an answer, if you ask the right question. Now ask me the question you want to know."

Tee-Tee took a few moments to think. "Who will replace Natasha, with us being one girl short?"

"We were never one girl short. We were always one girl over."

Tee-Tee thought about my answer and obviously wasn't happy with it. "Well, what will we use as our getaway vehicle?"

I put a sheepish grin on my face. "Let's just say, this heist will definitely make the papers, baby."

Chapter 8

The Super 8 Motel was a safe haven for orgies, drug deals, murders, prostitution and the likes. The three criminals thought they'd found nirvana. Chief was in one room selling weed, Big Meech was in another having a threesome, while Delano was in yet another getting his dick sucked by a toothless prostitute.

"Oooh shit, yeah! Wooo! Suck that shit just like that, no hands. Ahhh shit, yeah! I'm about to cum in your fuckin' mouth! Ahhhhh shit!" Delano exhaled, breathed heavily and smiled right before tossing the prostitute thirty dollars.

"Where the fuck is the other twenty?" the toothless Spanish chick asked him.

Delano thought about jerking her and putting her ass out his room, but she had just given him one of the best blowjobs he'd ever had, so he went back in his pockets and tossed another twenty-dollar bill to the floor, and she quickly scooped it up.

"No tip, muthafucka?" The feisty broad wiped cum from her chin.

"How about I put the tip of my dick in your ass?" Delano asked just as he got a text from Honey.

♠♠♠

"*Skunk* weed! Not punk weed!" Chief yelled at a middle-aged white customer. "Imported straight from New York. Ain't nobody on the West Coast got anything that can fuck with it."

The white dude eagerly pulled out a crisp hundred-dollar bill and handed it to Chief.

"My man!" Chief went into the bathroom and came back with a small Ziploc bag of weed and handed it to his investment banker client.

"You got any blow?"

"Not right now. That's on back order," Chief calmly explained.

The dude nodded his head and turned and exited the room.

"Yo, call me the *Chef* because I be serving them up!" Chief yelled out into the room as he counted a wad of cash. Just at that moment he got a text from Honey.

♠♠♠

Meanwhile Big Meech was being as reckless as he could possibly be. He was high off weed, but that was still no excuse for him to be running up raw in two white chicks. He had one white girl butt naked on her hands and knees on the floor, and he made the other butt naked white chick mount the white girl, so it looked as if one chick was giving the other a piggyback ride. He did that so that both of their asses could be facing him, giving him the perfect access he wanted.

The white girl who was on top turned and said to Big Meech, "Fuck me, daddy!"

Big Meech didn't need any urging as he fucked the white girl as hard as he could. Then without warning he pulled his dick out of her and he bent down and slipped his dick inside of the other white girl, who gasped as his dick entered her tight pussy.

Big Meech was feeling like he was just about to cum when he heard his phone on the table vibrating. He was going to ignore it, but he didn't know if it was Chief or Delano, and if they were in any kind of beef or anything.

Big Meech yelled, "Shit!" and he pulled his dick out of the white girl and walked over to his cell phone. He ignored the text from Honey and went right back to the white girls. Then he had them simultaneously suck his dick until he came.

All of the Super 8 Motel shenanigans came to an abrupt end when the three received the simultaneous texts from Honey. She was on her way and had called an emergency meeting. When she got there, no one was particularly happy to see her.

"Damn, Honey! I know this is your operation, but you can't think that when you say jump we're gonna say how high. We all had shit we was gettin' into," Chief stated.

"What's more important than tomorrow? Please riddle me that."

"I'm just saying, Couldn't this have waited?"

"Give her a break, Chief. You always ridin' her. If she came all the way down here, then it couldn't wait," Big Meech explained. "Go ahead, baby. School us," he said, even though his mind was on getting back to the two white chicks for another round of fucking.

♠♠♠

I wondered why it was so easy for Big Meech to respect me and not the mother of his only child. *Men. It's just too hard trying to figure them out.*

"A friend of mine is working the eleven to seven shift tonight, and I need all of you to show up around two a.m. and sit at her table and play a few hands—"

"That's gonna make us hot," Chief said. "Then we gotta come right back up in that bitch at seven? What's the logic?"

"As I was saying . . . the reason y'all need to come through is because the head of security, Javier needs to get a good look at all y'all faces."

Everyone screamed in unison, "What?"

"You jokin', right?"

"More serious than cancer."

"Yo, Honey, you tryin' to set us up or something?"

"I'm trying to get us home-court advantage. Javier is now on our team."

"Now we got another mutherfuckin' mouth to feed?" Chief retorted.

Big Meech immediately twisted up his face. "I don't trust him, Honey. Dude gonna set us up."

"All I know is that I'll be like Bobby DeNiro," Delano said. "I feel the heat coming around that corner, and I'll leave my momma out in the cold."

Chief began pacing up and down the cramped motel room. His action was making everyone nervous. "We didn't need him. Why you go and put him on to us?"

"Look, I got a friend back in the ATF who I called on a favor. When I did Javier's background check, he came up clean. When my friend ran his name, it pulled up his life story."

"So?"

"So? So he was dishonorably discharged from the U.S. Marines when he was nineteen for trying to steal a couple guns off base. No doubt, he would have sold them to his *hombres*. Next, he applied and got a job working for the Sheriff's Office in Orange County, California. Then he was fired for allegedly taking bribes under the table. That charge never stuck. He then moved out to Vegas and, using his mother's maiden name, became the head of security. That's why he came up clean."

Chief was barely listening. "What does any of this have to do with exposing ourselves to him?"

"Well, I got to thinking . . . I need to know the type of man who'll be holding down the casino when you run up in there. I need everyone to make it out alive. Now an ex-Marine, ex-cop just might want to play hero to redeem himself for all his wrongdoings. I couldn't take that chance, so I thought, A dirty muthafucka is a dirty muthafucka."

"Honey, take us around the block already! You takin' too long to get to the point."

Chief always did have a smart-ass mouth and dumb-ass brain, I thought.

"Bottom line is that Luther and I kidnapped his pregnant wife and two daughters two days ago. They're at an undisclosed location. He plays the game, they live. Along with five grand out of my cut."

I pulled out a photo of a Hispanic pregnant female and two young girls, all bound and gagged. Everyone inspected the picture.

"Damn, Honey! You really muthafuckin' hood!"

"I get down for mines," I replied. "I couldn't take a chance with this guy pulling a Rambo. Now with him on our team, when y'all run up in there, y'all don't gotta be so paranoid. That will leave Delano time to concentrate on helping retrieve the chips, instead of wasting the valuable three minutes keeping watch on Javier."

"Good plan, Honey. I like the way this is going down. And look at Luther. He still on his gangsta!" Chief said, cheering our work.

"I'm glad everyone is pleased with my decision."

"That's why you're the boss."

"Heavy lies the crown . . ." I replied aimlessly.

♠♠♠

At two o'clock we all headed to the blackjack table separately. I told them that no one would address each other—the dealer, Javier, no one. Everyone would act like we're strangers. We were there for one reason and one reason only.

"Yo, what's up with the wig?" Chief asked as I pulled on a short black wig and a pair of oversized shades.

"I work for the Bellagio, stupid."

"And?"

"And I'm supposed to be working tonight and tomorrow, but I called out sick. If someone bumps into me at Harrah's it could blow my whole cover."

"Oh, that's what's up. Well, ain't nobody gonna recognize you in that getup. I'm your blood and I don't even recognize you."

"That's why it's called a disguise." Before Chief could reply, I said, "Don't do it. Just let it hang out there in the universe. No need to even respond."

Shortly into our hand Javier walked over and greeted Kelly, the dealer for the evening. He took a quick, yet thorough glance at everyone and then kept it moving. He moved with ease, like a panther. Perhaps, more like a lion. He was strong and confident.

We all headed to our respective homes to rest up for our big day tomorrow. And what a day it was going to be. The last, most memorable day of all of our lives. A new beginning for some, doomsday for others. I didn't plan on getting much sleep, the details constantly replaying in my mind. If we were off by one minute, or if something unforeseeable occurred and we weren't ready to improvise, then tomorrow would become Armageddon. Tomorrow there was going to be one step between life and death, and I knew which side of the yellow tape I wanted to be on.

Chapter 9

You know Honey is gonna flip once she finds out that you've changed up the plan on her."

"I once heard that a lion doesn't concern himself with the opinions of lambs."

Big Meech laughed. "Oh, you a lion?"

"And then some," Chief replied. "It's about time somebody recognizes that shit."

"Nigga, you don't even know how to get paid. You got your little sister calling the shots. You ain't a shot-caller, partner."

"Tupac died a long time ago, homie. Who you be? One minute you this thug muthafucka, the next, you this little bitch taking orders from me. At least I'm consistent with mines."

Big Meech rose up toward Chief. Delano knew that things were about to escalate, yet he couldn't think of anything to do to quell the situation. He was hoping his words would suffice. "Y'all niggas need to be easy. This time tomorrow night we'll all be rich as hell."

Both men ignored Delano's weak attempt at a distraction.

"Who the fuck you calling a bitch, pussy?"

Chief was tired of bigger niggas always trying him because of his size. "Fuck all that dumb shit you talkin', you bitch-ass nigga! You don't got balls between your legs that's straight pussy! I was graduating the school of 'get money,' while you were still on your fifth year of high school."

Big Meech's massive hands grabbed Chief up by the throat, lifting him three feet in the air, feet dangling. Chief, losing oxygen by the second, desperately tried to claw at Big Meech's hands and face to no avail.

"Meech, come on now. You're gonna kill dude!" Delano barked. "It ain't worth it. It's only words."

But it was much more to Big Meech. He refused to be disrespected. By anyone. Especially a puny wannabe who never put in any real work. Big Meech was the muscle, and as far as he was concerned, if it weren't for him, Chief wouldn't have had half the shit he had, including his life. Meech had put a lot of niggas to sleep for Chief, and now he was being disrespected by some low-level ingrate.

Right before Chief was about to lose consciousness, he pulled his pistol from his waist and shot Big Meech in his kneecap. The sound echoed throughout the room. Instantly Chief dropped to the floor, gasping for air.

"You shot me, muthafucka?" Big Meech asked, his knee throbbing. As the blood squirted, oozed and dripped down his injured leg, all he could think about was killing Chief with his bare hands.

Delano stayed mute. He knew the situation could only get worse. They were in Chief's motel room, and he was the only one packing heat. Delano feared if he said the wrong thing that he too would catch a bullet. That, coupled with the fear that five-O would come kicking in the door, made his stomach queasy. Not because he'd never been locked down before because he had. But because they were all so close to pulling off the perfect heist and walking away with millions in a matter of ninety seconds. He wanted that paper so badly that he'd already begun spending it in his mind. He knew that was taboo, but all he envisioned was the shiny, black-on-black Range Rover with custom seats. He wanted silver piping around the black butter-soft leather seats and his initials in each headrest. Next, he needed the 18-inch rose gold chain with a 5-carat cross that dangled near his dick. And he did want a platinum Rolex. He had a gold Rolex Presidential back in the day that he'd robbed some Wall Street dude of, but pawned when times got hard. Now all he sported was a waterproof Gucci Sport, which didn't exactly represent that of a baller. All his dreams of grandeur were going down the drain, and he couldn't do a damn thing about it.

Slowly Chief began to regain his strength. He took one look at Big Meech and knew he'd fucked up. What was he going to do now? They needed Big Meech for tomorrow.

"You don't look so good," Chief said, almost in disbelief. He observed that Big Meech's face looked clammy and he was sweating profusely. He also recognized that blood was pouring out of him by the bucket from one little gunshot wound. "Help him!"

Delano snapped out of his zone and ran to the bathroom and grabbed a few towels to soak up the blood.

"I'm feeling lightheaded," Big Meech said, before collapsing on the side of the bed. "You did a nigga dirty."

"You know I didn't mean that shit. Fuck you wanted a nigga to do?" Chief took off his T-shirt and tied it around Big Meech's leg to try and stop the bleeding. "Let you choke me out?"

"Y'all gotta take me to the hospital, or I ain't gonna make it," Big Meech said, his voice strained and filled with concern. "I think you hit an artery."

"I ain't hit no artery, man. You just paranoid, that's all."

"At this stage only the paranoid survives, Chief. I'm tellin' you, man, I ain't gonna make it."

"Stop with that foolishness and let me think. You know, if we take you to the hospital, it's gonna make us hot."

"Just drop me out front, homie. I ain't new to this. You know I ain't on no snitchin' shit."

"Chief, why are we even debating this? Man, we gotta get him to the hospital. Dude fucked up."

Chief looked down at his dying friend. As far as he was concerned, Big Meech had brought the events upon himself.

"Meech, you gotta charge this one to the game, man. You already dead." Chief stepped back and absorbed his words. "No telling what could happen to me and Delano during the transport. What if we get pulled over? You know we could get knocked over your bullshit."

"Chief, don't do this, man. I'm begging you. Delano, talk some sense into him please."

Delano weighed his options. Big Meech was his man, but Chief was brandishing the pistol. Besides, most of what Chief had said was true. Big Meech did bring it upon himself. Words were words, but you can't just choke out a nigga and think it's all love. And what if they piled Big Meech into the car and tried to transport him on these hot Las Vegas streets and he died before they made it to the hospital? What if they got pulled over by the cops with his dead body in the backseat? How could they explain shit away? They'd both get locked up on a murder rap, but most importantly there'd be no heist.

When Delano didn't come to his defense, Big Meech said, "Y'all know y'all can't do the heist without me. There's no way it would work. It ain't a two-man job. Take me to the hospital and let them stitch me back together. I'll be out in two days." Big Meech had to catch his breath. He felt like any second he was about to lose consciousness. "We could reschedule the heist for next week. It's only a minor hiccup"—Big Meech could no longer keep his eyes open. Slowly they closed, and he slumped forward.

"That nigga gone, yo," Chief said. "Now what?"

"You tell me."

"A nigga ain't good at improvising." Chief began to tap the gun on the side of his head. "His big ass too heavy to move, especially now that he's deadweight. We shoulda made his ass limp to the car."

"Should we have made him dig his own grave too?" Delano asked dryly.

Chief didn't like Delano's sarcasm. He knew that Delano would be a wild card. Once things were over, Chief would never be able to trust him. Surely, Delano would want to dead him first chance he got. At that moment, Chief was already plotting Delano's date of death.

"Don't run that guilt trip on me. I didn't see you doing shit to help your man. He asked you too to get him to the hospital. I ain't see you make a move, so you got blood on your hands just like me."

Delano wanted to respond. He looked down at Big Meech slumped, leaning against a dirty mattress in a cheap motel, and wondered how a bullet to the knee could take out such a formable man within a matter of five minutes. It was unreal. He knew dudes who took nine shots and lived.

Delano decided not to beef over spilt milk. "Yo, ain't no way we gonna be able to carry his big ass down these two flights of steps, into the trunk of the car, and then unload him to dump in the desert."

Chief almost boiled over. "Tell me something I don't fuckin' know!"

Delano exhaled. He hated to say it, but he did. "Let's call Honey."

♠♠♠

Honey arrived at the scene of the crime, and once again she had to clean up her brother's mess. It was 4:40 a.m., just hours before their big heist, and she was standing inches away from an almost dead body. She touched his carotid artery. His breathing was shallow. "You know he's still alive, right?"

"Hell no, we didn't know," Chief replied. "But that don't mean shit. There ain't nothing we can do for him. He fucked up."

Honey agreed. She'd just thought that they wanted to know the facts.

"I got six jugs of five gallons of gasoline in my trunk. That's all I was able to get at such short notice."

"Gasoline? We gonna burn his body?"

"Y'all gonna torch this bitch—the whole Super 8. But first go and gather up all your belongings. Don't leave even your toothbrush. Load everything up in your trunk." Honey tossed them each a pair of gloves. "Wipe down each room. Grab all the sheets and towels and place it in the middle of the floor and saturate each pile with the gasoline. Douse the chairs, television, and desks. And y'all might want to do your friend a solid and put him out of his misery. One to the dome would be nice, but you can't risk someone hearing that shot. Y'all are resourceful. I'm sure you'll figure it out before you burn him alive."

Chief asked, "Why not just soak the mattress?"

"Because hotel mattresses are lined with fire retardant material. It delays a fire from spreading, just in case someone falls asleep smoking in bed."

"Oh, that's what's up."

"Look, I don't have time for twenty questions. Do as I say, and we can still be millionaires in three hours. Y'all got less than an hour to torch this bitch and make it to the casino by seven a.m. Can y'all handle that?"

"But we one man down," Chief replied.

"Thank you for the revelation. Thank God y'all got Javier on y'all side, or else we'd all be fucked."

Both men suddenly felt energized. They'd forgotten about Javier. Delano didn't have to back him down and would be free to help bag up the chips.

Chief and Delano both began running around from room to room doing as Honey said. And when they doused their partner in crime with gasoline, neither bothered to make sure he was dead before striking the match.

The Crime

♣ Erica Hilton ♣

crime (krm)
n.

*1. An act committed or omitted in violation
of a law forbidding or commanding it and for
which punishment is imposed upon conviction.*

2. Unlawful activity: statistics relating to violent crime.

3. A serious offense, especially one in violation of morality.

*4. An unjust, senseless, or disgraceful act or condition:
It's a crime to squander our country's natural resources.*

Chapter 10

After torching the motel, Chief and Delano scrambled to get away. It would take at least an hour for the fire to gain momentum and spread throughout each room. By that time the pair had hoped they'd be finished with their heist and on their way back to New York. Chief couldn't wait to touch down in his hometown. Vegas wasn't his thing. It was a great place to spend a vacation, but to live was a whole different beast. Too many different walks of life all cramped into one environment and rubbing elbows with each other on a day-to-day basis—hood dudes sprinkled throughout the "Esses," Mexican gang members from Los Angeles; country bumpkins; the Mafioso; playboy-bunny types; and the straight-laced corporate guy.

Chief loved walking to the local bodega to get a ham-and-cheese sandwich and tossing that back with a Red Bull early in the morning. Standing on his corner, gun tucked in his waist, and kicking it with his dudes, who all spoke the same language, that made him feel comfortable and secure.

"Hurry up, man. Drive this muthafucka. We only got a few minutes to pick up Luther so we can go and set this muthafucka off!"

Delano was a little tired, not only fatigued from a night of no sleep, but from Chief's constant bullshit. He was always barking orders, like his shit don't stink. Had it not been for him taking out Big Meech last night, they wouldn't be running so far behind. And he wasn't about to get pulled over, dirty, in Vegas. Chief just didn't use his head.

"I gotta do the speed limit, man. We can't blow it when we're this close."

Chief sucked his teeth. "Man, fuck all that speed limit shit!" Chief was agitated, the way he always felt right before committing a crime. His nerves always got the better of him. "The last thing I want to hear is Luther's mouth when we pull up late."

Delano ignored Chief for the rest of the ride and just concentrated on the road. He knew that sooner than later he'd make Chief disappear. Payback for a lot of unnecessary shit he'd pulled throughout the years.

When the two reached Luther, he was already standing out front smoking a cigarette. They were only five minutes late, but Luther's expression showed that he wasn't too pleased.

Luther ordered Delano, "Get in the back," and took the wheel.

As Luther drove, both Chief and Delano began checking and rechecking their pistols to make sure there was a bullet in every chamber and that their guns were off the safety latch. The click-clacking of guns wasn't new to Luther's ears.

"So, y'all good with the plan, right?" Luther asked.

No one answered. Chief was still upset that he had to follow Honey's plan. Honey didn't know it, but right before he and Big Meech had gotten into it, Chief had changed the plan. He no longer wanted to rob the casino for chips, thinking that was low-level stuff. He wanted to rob the armored car that was dropping off the chips—make it up close and personal. He wanted it to be cowboys and Indians playing out on the Las Vegas streets. There was something about Honey's plan that didn't sit too well with him. He knew his sister. He knew she was sneaky, but he couldn't put his finger on what she was up to. And right now it didn't matter because he was riding three-deep to carry out his sister's wishes.

When they pulled up, they saw the stolen FedEx minivan with Cinnamon behind the wheel, drinking coffee and eating a donut. There was so much early-morning commotion going on at the hotel's entrance, she blended in perfectly as Honey said she would. She had no idea that her baby daddy was shot and burned alive only hours ago.

♣ ♣ ♣

The Garda armored truck passed its early morning inspection, and the three guards, Michael, Jeffrey, and Elizabeth all loaded up and were ready to go. Today was a typical Wednesday, uneventful for the crew. They had to make four casino stops, one Walmart, and three ATM machines before returning back to base just before three p.m.

Elizabeth usually took the wheel, but Jeffrey had complained of back troubles due to late-night bowling, so she agreed to ride shotgun. It was exactly seven a.m. when they pulled out.

"Did you hear about Obama catching Bin Laden?" Elizabeth, a die-hard Democrat asked.

"I heard that our U.S. Navy Seals captured and murdered Bin Laden. Is that the story you're referring to?"

Jeffrey was a conservative Republican who wanted Sarah Palin to run in the upcoming election and win. He was born and raised in Mississippi where they still fly the Confederate flag and you were taught to shoot first and ask questions next. He loved few things in life—his country, his job, and his whiskey.

"Well, whoever you want to give credit to, the fact still remains that he's dead, which is good for our country all around."

"I'm not going to debate you on that, but the true credit goes to the Bush administration. G.W. put the plan in motion after 9/11, and the Seals just carried it out."

"Now you sound like Fox News." Elizabeth rolled her eyes and grabbed for the receiver. "Base this is car 790. Radio check, route 3, routine. We're approaching the side entrance of Harrah's Casino, making our first stop of the day. Copy."

Static rippled through the air and then, "Car 790, are you clear? Copy."

"Yes, sir. Radio check in fifteen minutes. Copy."

"Copy that."

Jeffrey pulled along the side of the loading dock. When the car came to a complete stop, Elizabeth exited it first, hand hovering over her pistol, something she'd learned the first week in training. Before motioning for Michael to open up the back door of the truck, she scanned the perimeter. Nothing seemed suspicious. She gave the code: two knocks on the back door and then, "All clear."

Michael was ready for action. He was pumped up off two cups of coffee and excited about this evening. He had tickets to the Phoenix Suns against the Miami Heat summer league game, which took place every summer in Las Vegas, showcasing NBA teams' top rookie talent. His new girlfriend had bought him two tickets on the condition that she accompany him. She wouldn't have been his first choice, or even his second, but since she did make the purchase, who was he to complain.

Elizabeth and Michael didn't talk much while they were unloading the large sums of casino chips out of the truck. They were very professional and knew that their lives were at stake whenever they were in the field. One false move and they wouldn't make it home for supper.

Both took turns carrying over eighty pounds of chips into the side entrance and into the secure hands of Harrah's Casino security, while Jeffrey held his position as the third set of eyes.

So far so good, Jeffrey thought. Until an ordinary Nissan Maxima pulled up with three black guys, an older gentleman at the wheel and two younger gentlemen. Jeffrey watched as they all peered down the alley in his direction.

Are they looking at me? he thought. "What are you monkeys looking at?" he said out loud to himself.

The two passengers continually looked around. There seemed to be a lot of commotion going on in the small car so early in the morning. He thought they were about to have some action. Jeffrey was just about to radio for backup when the two passengers exited the vehicle and walked in the opposite direction of his armored car. He figured they were going inside the casino to gamble. When the driver backed his car up and drove off, he knew he had been reaching for straws.

He laughed out loud. "What an idiot I am."

At approximately 7:50 a.m., Michael and Elizabeth were safely inside the truck and on their way to their next drop-off location. The Wynn Hotel and Casino was just minutes up the strip.

♣ ♣ ♣

Luther peeled away from the side entrance of the casino right on time. He peered down at his watch and knew that soon Honey and her girls would be approaching the Bellagio. They all had strict instructions to not use cell phones. Otherwise, he would have called her to tell her how downright obvious Chief and Delano were. They were the most paranoid criminals he'd ever met. He had to scream on them several times to stop looking at the armored car driver. He was so glad his part of the heist was almost complete.

♣ ♣ ♣

Chief and Delano casually walked into Harrah's Casino and headed toward separate tables, just as planned. Chief hit the baccarat, and Delano found the craps table. Though they'd walked in at almost eight in the morning, the crowded, noisy atmosphere felt more like eleven at night, with slot machines going off every second and little old ladies dropping quarter after quarter, hoping to win big.

Chief passed by Javier and saw him do a slight head nod. He had almost forgotten that Javier's wife and kids were held hostage. Not that he felt any sympathy, but it was an issue.

Immediately Chief joined in the action. He peered over at the bank and counted at least a million dollars in chips. You had to buy in at one hundred dollars, and the chips ranged from one hundred to one thousand dollars. Chief concluded it would take him less than thirty seconds to dump those chips in his bag and bounce. He was confident that his Aviator shades, fitted baseball cap, and scruffy mustache and beard he'd grown was enough to shield his identity. But, honestly, he didn't care. He loved living on the edge. Once this heist made the papers, it would take him a matter of days before he began bragging about it back in Brooklyn. What good was getting away with a crime if no one knew you were the one who'd done it? Part of the glory was the bragging. That's what legends are made of—the backstory.

♣ ♣ ♣

Delano was getting antsy. He felt they needed Big Meech. He'd never done a heist of this magnitude, and with only Chief and the promise of the backup of Javier, someone he'd never broken bread with, had made him more than just a little paranoid. He'd tried to concentrate on the table and not bring too much suspicion on himself until he needed to pull out his gat, but he ended up doing exactly what Honey had warned them not to do—looking up at the cameras and fidgeting.

As he looked around, it appeared that everyone was watching him. Did they all know? Had Javier dropped dime? He didn't have a good feeling at all. What if the lady to his right was undercover? Or the man to his left FBI? It was one thing to get knocked for a robbery—he'd be out in three to five—but kidnapping a woman and her two kids held a life sentence. Was he in too deep?

"Sir, it's your roll," the dealer stated to Delano.

Everyone stared impatiently because he was holding up their momentum. Delano rolled.

"Snake eyes. You lose." The dealer swooped up the dice and the chips.

Delano began to get hot under his collar. Snake eyes? Was that an omen? He looked over and Chief looked cooler than a cucumber. They had less than five minutes to strike, but Delano was feeling squeamish.

Chief didn't see Delano coming, but when he tapped him on the shoulder, he wanted to shit in his pants. His face turned beet-red from aggravation. "Yo, what are you doing?" Chief whispered through clenched teeth.

"Chief, fam, I'm not feeling this. Something ain't right."

"You just nervous because Meech ain't here. Don't worry, man, I got you. Just play your part, and we gonna make it outta here paid in full." Chief turned his back on Delano as to not hear anymore nonsense. He thought that gesture, and pep talk would force him to go back to his station and prepare for the inevitable.

Instead, Delano began to backpedal away from Chief then spun around and almost bolted toward the front door. He wanted to get Luther to go in and talk some sense into Chief.

The blazing hot sun immediately snatched Delano's breath away after leaving the air conditioning in the luxury casino. His eyes scanned the perimeter, and no longer did he see the FedEx getaway van. *Where the fuck is Cinnamon? She knew better than to move the vehicle,* he thought. The heist was to jump off any second. He wanted to reach into his knapsack and get on his walkie-talkie, but that would've drawn too much attention.

Briskly Delano walked to the left of the driveway and then doubled back and walked right. That's when it dawned on him that Luther was nowhere around either. *How the fuck are we supposed to get away from the scene of the crime without a getaway form of transportation?*

Delano's gut couldn't figure out what was up, but he knew it wasn't good. One part of him wanted to take off on foot, maybe hitchhike to the nearest bus station, but the hood in him was calling.

Delano turned right back around and marched back into the casino. *Fuck it*, he thought. *I'd rather go out a soldier than run like a bitch.*

♣ ♣ ♣

Chief turned around and all he saw was Delano's backside making a beeline toward the front door. "Look at this punk muthafucka," he said underneath his breath.

Chief had two minutes to debate what he was going to do. How could he single-handedly rob the casino? That would be virtually impossible. He thought for a second. It would be difficult but not impossible, he reasoned, because Javier was holding him down. There wouldn't be any security to stop him, and his getaway driver and distraction were out front counting on him. He could only imagine everyone's face when he burst out the front door solo, carrying his knapsack full of chips. Honey and Luther would no longer be able to call him a dumb criminal.

He knew he had to set it off. He pulled out his gat and let off one shot in the air. "Nobody fuckin' move, nobody gets hurt!"

The screams and pandemonium could be heard for blocks. Everyone was being trampled, trying to run for cover.

"Not you my friend!" Chief pushed the gun into the dealer's side. "Load this muthafucka with chips! Now!"

The petrified dealer did as he was told, his hands moving with accuracy. The last thing he wanted was a bullet in the gut, and the threatening look in the robber's eyes said that he meant business.

In less than forty seconds Chief had a knapsack with nearly one million dollars of casino chips resting on his back.

"Put the gun down, or we'll shoot!" Javier screamed, his gun aimed directly at Chief's head. He and six armed security guards surrounded Chief with automatic weapons.

"Yo, Javier, man, this ain't part of the plan. Whatchu doin', homie?"

"I ain't your homie. Now put down your weapon!"

"You know, if I don't make it out of here alive, neither does your wife and kids."

Javier looked perplexed. "I'm not married, muthafucka! And I ain't got no fuckin' kids! Now put the gun down! I won't ask you again!"

Alarms began ringing off in Chief's head. He knew he'd just walked into a trap, but what he couldn't answer was why, and how many people were involved in setting him up to get knocked or possibly worse.

"Either put down your gat, or I'll let you go without your head!" Delano had snuck up behind the unsuspecting Javier and had gotten the drop on him. He had yoked Javier up and was using his body as a shield from his security team. "Tell your goons to drop their weapons."

Javier, now with his life at stake, told his men, "Stand down, goddamnit!" he barked when one security guard seemed like he wanted to be a hero.

Javier was five years away from a full pension and he refused to get murdered and let his greedy sister, his next of kin, reap all his benefits while he rotted in a grave. The casino had insurance, which was enough to make his decision easier.

"Boy, I've never been happier to see someone in my life!" Chief screamed. He went around gathering up every guard's gun and then removing each clip.

Delano then tossed him his knapsack, and Chief loaded his up as well.

"You know we got setup, don't you?" Delano said, with a firm grip on Javier.

"Yeah! I thought you were one of the muthafuckas who set me up. But you ain't said nothing but a word. We're gonna kill each and every one of them, starting with Honey."

An off-duty Las Vegas metro police officer who had been playing craps just minutes earlier was watching everything unfold and was waiting to make a move on Chief and Delano. The officer had been trained just for situations like this. The first thing he did was secretly send out a text message to his entire list of cop friends telling them to send a SWAT team ASAP, and that he was not joking. He then dialed 911, and whispered into the phone. "Harrah's Casino is being robbed at gun point. Send help."

After he left that message, Chief was just about finished loading his knapsack. That was when the officer made his move and sprang into action. "LVPD! Drop your weapons!" he ordered, his police-issued 9mm handgun aimed at Chief and Delano.

Chief panicked, but he didn't hesitate to fire his gun.

Blaow! Blaow! Blaow!

Chief's three shots at the officer forced him to take cover.

"Bounce! Go, go, go!" Chief ordered Delano to leave with Javier, while he continued to provide cover for him by firing at the officer, who was ducked down behind the huge craps table. There was so much firepower, an exchange of live rounds being fired that the sounds echoed throughout the casino. Harrah's looked like a kill zone so many people were down.

"Don't crap out, muthafucka. Police bleed red just like I do. Don't be a fuckin' hero." Chief then fired more shots as Delano and Javier made their way out of the casino.

The officer spoke into his cell phone, "Hello, hello. Yeah, this is off-duty officer Mike Fox. I'm calling from inside Harrah's Casino. We got a robbery in progress, multiple shots fired, a possible hostage situation. Two armed black male perps both dark-skin and both approximately six feet tall and two hundred pounds wearing dark-colored athletic wear. One has braids, and the other is bald. Send SWAT and send every unit you have. And get a bus over here right away as there may be gunshot victims."

He then peered around the craps table and saw Delano and Chief making their escape. There was a rising sense of panic, but he had to do what he had to do to stop them. He started to give chase. He had one clear shot at the suspects, but he had to hold his fire because there were too many innocent bystanders in the casino who could have been harmed by his bullets. He also knew that Delano had a hostage, so he really had to be careful.

Once again Chief peered out his peripheral vision and noticed the cop was still in pursuit. "Blaow! Blaow! Blaow!—" Chief let off a succession of gunshots. An innocent bystander took one in the gut. The avid poker player looked down and touched his belly. It felt like a bowl of jelly as his insides spilled out. The sheer terror at the realization of having been shot caused the wounded man to faint. He was a pitiful sight.

In a matter of minutes, if not seconds, every cop in Las Vegas and all of the surroundings counties would be arriving to give him assistance.

♣ ♣ ♣

Las Vegas, Nevada was a busy, crowded city. A perfect storm of distractions to keep authorities baffled while executing the crime of the century. Honey sat listening to the police scanner. It was just six past eight in the morning. So far, nothing. She almost thought that her meticulous plan had a flaw.

Then she heard, "Attention all cars! Attention all cars! We got a possible two-eleven in progress. Multiple shots fired at Harrah's Casino! We need all units to head to Harrah's Casino. Two armed black male perps, both dark-skinned and approximately six feet tall and weighing two hundred pounds. One perp has braids, and one is bald. Perps may have one hostage. Be on the lookout for off-duty officer Mike Fox, who is on location and pursuing the two perps."

"Let's do it," Honey demanded.

Honey and Mercedes jumped on separate lime-green and black Ducati motorcycles, while Tee-Tee, Blythe, and Party piled into a late-model Toyota Camry. The girls all jumped on Interstate 15, headed toward the Bellagio Hotel and Casino just as planned.

"How's everyone feeling this morning?" Honey asked, testing the Bluetooth's.

Mercedes came in loud and clear. "I'm ready for action."

"Good to hear. What about you, Tee-Tee? You good?"

"I'm better than ever, Honey. Will be even better in a couple hours."

"I know that's right," Honey replied.

Honey's heart was pounding as she neared the Bellagio, dressed in an all-black jumpsuit, money colored green bandana tied around her left arm, black gloves, and black helmet. So much was at stake. She was responsible for so many lives, and one false move could cost everyone everything.

♣ ♣ ♣

The Brinks security truck backed into the loading dock of the Bellagio Hotel, the siren sounding a warning for all those in the way to move. Slowly, the skilled driver came to a complete stop. Jamal jumped out of the passenger's side door and made his way to the back. Today was his second week on the job, and so far, so good. He was working with a skilled team that had taken its time in showing him the ropes.

At twenty-two years old, he wanted to finish college and get a job as an engineer. But when his high school sweetheart had turned up pregnant, he had to drop out of college and grab a job to help make ends meet. His plan was to re-enroll next semester for night classes.

Jamal tapped on the glass. "All clear!" he said.

His partner opened up without trepidation. He was a twenty-year armored car veteran, and he was only forty-one.

As the unsuspecting Jamal began to unload their truck, Mercedes yelled in her thick Mexican accent, "Don't move, muthafucka!"

Her accent alone is intimidating, Honey thought.

When the veteran guard turned around to face Mercedes with his hands held up high, she immediately recognized his face. Mercedes knew she was supposed to put one in his dome, but this was the same guy she had seen with Honey just a few nights earlier. Was there a mistake? Were her eyes playing tricks on her? So many thoughts were running through her head, leaving her confused. What if she took the shot and wasn't supposed to? What if something crazy had happened to put this guy in the wrong place at the wrong time? Did Honey know her lover worked for Brinks?

Honey's TEC-9 exploded. *Blaow!*

When Mercedes didn't take the shot, Honey realized that she must've recognized Brian from the other night. Honey knew to always go with her gut. She thought that Mercedes had gotten a good look at Brian but tried to tell herself differently.

Both women watched as his body hit the hot, dirty pavement like a sack of potatoes.

"Set it off!" Honey screamed, and each girl began putting in work.

Party instantly took out the driver with a deadly shot to the right side of his neck. Blood squirted out of the hole, and he let out an agonizing scream. He tried to reach for his pistol, but she put one in his left temple with the accuracy of a skilled marksman.

Mercedes didn't want to be left out. When the third guard, Jamal, dropped down to his knees in surrender, she didn't have a choice. She knew they couldn't leave any witnesses. She put one shot in the back of his head and then looked to Honey, who gave her a quick nod of approval.

The stragglers and employees began scattering and running for cover. Everyone ran away from the casino, hoping to not get hit by any stray bullets.

Honey saw a few familiar faces, but only one lingered longer than necessary. Rosie from housekeeping. For some odd reason she glared in Honey's direction. Honey had two seconds to react. She adjusted her stiff neck from side to side and then lifted her TEC-9, but Rosie took off, wobbling down the block. Honey could have taken the shot, but inexplicably she didn't. It was too early in the morning for killing coworkers.

Tee-Tee and Blythe were ordered to hold down the back entrance, while Honey, Mercedes, and Party were moving like robots, unloading the armored car and loading the FedEx minivan that Cinnamon was driving. Simultaneously, they all began grabbing up the heavy bags of dough, each bag weighing at least sixty pounds, and walking them several yards away. The minivan was parked in a blind spot where it wouldn't be picked up by video surveillance. This process of walking the money to the FedEx minivan cost them valuable time, but it was a necessary maneuver to ensure that the vehicle carrying the dough wouldn't get tailed.

Cinnamon nervously sat perched behind the helm, her fingers gripping the steering wheel so tight, her pink flesh turned white.

Tee-Tee and Blythe anticipated that at any second a slew of armed guards would come barreling out the back doors. Between the video surveillance cameras, the shots fired, and the screaming bystanders, it was only a matter of moments. All this mayhem had taken a matter of minutes.

Once the minivan was loaded up, Honey tapped the side, "Go! Go! Go!" and Cinnamon peeled out of the lot.

♣ ♣ ♣

Chief and Delano was almost to the front door when a second set of armed guards came running from the back of the casino. Neither one of these guards was prepared to stand down. Nor did they seem to care that their boss was being used as a shield.

"Freeze! Don't move, muthafuckas!" one guard yelled.

"Wait! N-n-n-noooo!" Javier yelled.

Delano put one in Javier's temple. He needed agility if he was going to make it out of there alive.

Immediately Chief pulled out his second gat and began firing both pistols at the army of guards' bullet for bullet. Though Chief and Delano were outnumbered and outgunned two to seventeen, they weren't going out without a good fight.

♣ ♣ ♣

Hotel security had made its way to the back of the Bellagio Casino the instant the cameras picked up the heist in progress. Just as the back doors burst open, Honey spun around first and sprayed the walkway with a barrage of bullets from her TEC-9, backing them all up. They all retreated back inside the casino and ran around to the side entrance, which bought Honey and her crew time.

"Tee-Tee, you and Blythe cover the north and south entrances. I'll remain here and cover the back! You got thirty seconds to get the fuck outta here!" Honey reloaded her clip. Shit was getting thick. She could hear Party telling her through the Bluetooth that she was headed toward the getaway vehicle and would spin around to pickup Tee-Tee and Blythe. Honey ordered Mercedes to bounce.

"But what about you?" Mercedes asked, not wanting to leave Honey alone.

"Don't worry about me. I need to cover the back until Party picks up Tee-Tee and Blythe. Hurry the fuck up, ladies! The clock is ticking. Y'all got twenty seconds and counting! Mercedes, get your ass outta here! You got two kids, bitch. Move your ass!"

Mercedes hopped on her Ducati, took one last look at her crew, and peeled out. She nearly crashed head-on into a black Range Rover as she sped down Las Vegas Boulevard, her heart palpitating at a hundred beats a second, but she quickly regained control.

♣ ♣ ♣

Once outside Chief realized what Delano already knew—They didn't have a getaway vehicle. He could hear the faint sound of sirens getting louder. He looked over his shoulder and saw a couple just exiting their vehicle with California plates. They had two teenage girls with them and was unaware that a heist had just taken place. The engine of the shiny Lexus was still running.

"Get the fuck back in the car!" Chief brandished his weapon in the male's face.

His eyes popped open in horror. "Please don't hurt us!" he screamed.

"Shut the fuck up!" Chief barked. "Delano, grab the wheel."

Delano grabbed the wife by the back of her neck and shoved her into the passenger seat, with Chief, the father, and two teenagers crammed in the back.

Before Delano could get behind the wheel of the car, Harrah's driveway was swarmed with cop cars, SWAT, and now hotel and casino security. It was a scene right out of a movie. Helicopters were hovering over the grounds, and all law enforcement had their weapons drawn.

"Put your faces in the back windows, or I'll blow your muthafuckin' brains out!" Chief demanded.

The hostages did as they were told. Immediately, the daughters began crying.

"Shut the fuck up, bitches!" Chief ordered. Beads of perspiration had begun to form around his hairline and randomly drip salty sweat into his eyes. "Y'all better shut up, or I'll shut you up permanently!"

Instantly the cries turned into soft whimpers.

The father tried to console his girls as best as he could. "Shhhhh! Look at Daddy. It'll be OK, I promise you. Just be brave."

With the back window wallpapered with innocent faces, the police chief ordered his men to hold their fire, allowing Delano to get behind the wheel and take off down Las Vegas Boulevard with thirty police vehicles and SWAT tailing, and two helicopters hovering overhead.

♣ ♣ ♣

In the opposite direction of Las Vegas Boulevard, Honey had to make her own getaway. As promised, she held down the back entrance of the casino just waiting for someone to open up the door. She was ready to let off her TEC once again. Checking her peripheral vision, she could see that Party had spun the car around and had safely picked up Blythe, but when she made her way to Tee-Tee, a host of security guards opened fired. Automatic weapons and revolvers let off numerous shots, and Tee-Tee took one for the team.

Doubling over in sheer pain, Tee-Tee clutched her abdomen in an effort to stop the bleeding. Honey ran and jumped on her sleek Ducati and sped over to assist. Blythe jumped out blazing but had to lower her weapon in an effort to drag Tee-Tee in the car.

"Hurry up!" Party yelled, as she opened fired to cover Blythe.

Blythe was moving as fast as she could, but with bullets flying just inches above her head, that task was harder than it looked. Her armpits and hands instantly were drenched in sweat.

Party saw Honey speeding toward them. Honey leaned her bike toward the right and, with the TEC on her left, let out a hail of bullets, injuring several security guards and forcing the others to retreat.

♣ ♣ ♣

Inside, security continued to call for backup.

"Where the fuck is Las Vegas police?" one guard yelled on the walkie-talkie. "We're getting killed out here!"

There was static and then, "We've notified the police, but they've been held up over at Harrah's. There isn't anyone else on duty. They're trying to find a car to send over."

"No cars?" the guard said. "What the fuck you mean? My men are fuckin' dyin' out here!"

"Just remain calm. Help is on the way," the dispatcher said.

♣ ♣ ♣

Finally Honey and her crew were able to make a clean getaway. Honey watched as Party hopped on Interstate 15, while she veered off and took the side streets.

Under an overpass, just minutes from the Bellagio, Honey pulled over, and that's where she met Luther waiting for her in her vehicle. He'd been listening to the police scanner and was more than thankful when he saw his daughter.

Honey quickly pulled off her motorcycle helmet and stripped out of the one-piece jumpsuit, her Bellagio uniform underneath. Slipping on her heels that were on the passenger's seat, she said, "Tee-Tee was hit. All others clear. You're on cleanup patrol. I'll meet you tonight."

Luther nodded. He watched Honey make a right and head back to the Bellagio. Within seconds he had torched the bike and went into part three of the plan. Just feet away was a smelly old shopping cart with bottles and cans. He put on the tattered and torn overcoat and simply pushed his cart down E. Flamingo Road and blended in.

♣ ♣ ♣

The streets were now littered with bystanders looking up in the sky. The helicopters were broadcasting live from the Harrah's heist and had seemingly neglected the Bellagio, just as Honey had planned.

Honey reached the casino at approximately the right time. Two cop cars had finally arrived along with fire trucks and three ambulance vehicles. She slid in just before they began cordoning off the property and not allowing anyone else in. She needed to be seen shortly after the robbery, or her name would've been placed on the list of possible suspects.

She ran to her supervisor, Alonzo, "What's going on?"

"Not now, Honey! The casino's been fuckin' hit!" He brushed past her and made his way to the back.

Honey made her way to the back entrance, shoving and pushing her way through pedestrians. There she saw the gruesome scene she'd just taken part in. Three bodies lay dead, cooking in the hot Nevada sun. She looked down at her lover Brian. The married Brian who actually thought he was down with the heist. She wondered what his thoughts were once that bullet hit his head. Did he realize that he'd been used, when all along he thought he was using her?

It was Brian who'd approached Honey about the heist last year. She was new to the casino and had mistakenly given herself away when she was at a shooting range and had shot out the mark's face. When the guy at the range asked how she'd become such a great marksman, she told him she was former ATF.

Only, she didn't know Brian was in the next booth and had overheard the conversation. The next day, he found her at her blackjack table and began courting her. Right after a night of sweaty sex, he casually brought up the idea. Honey listened. She knew she was only a stepping stone for him. She also knew that, the moment the heist was done, he'd put a bullet in the back of her head and go and spend his dirty money with his wife and kids.

As the coroner pronounced each victim dead on the scene, a white blanket was thrown over each one after their bodies were outlined in chalk. Newscasters and cameras began flooding the area and reporting live from the scene of the crime.

Honey looked around and saw several females crying their eyes out. She wondered if she should cry too. She closed her eyes tight and tried to force out the tears, but nothing came. She then tried to rub her eyes roughly. Still nothing. Finally, she brought out the big guns and thought about her mother, and bingo! A full-on waterfall.

The next thing she knew, she was being comforted by several of her coworkers. Honey had a calculating gaze that convinced people to trust her. A vulnerability mixed with innocence.

"How could something like this happen?" she asked, looking up into several concerned eyes.

"People are so heartless. These men had families," one coworker said.

"None of us are safe," Honey replied. "What if we were coming into that back door at the time of the robbery? We could have been killed."

"You know, Rosie from housekeeping and Jasmine the barmaid said they were there when it all went down."

"Really?" Honey's interest was piqued. "What did they say they saw?"

"I don't know. The police have them now, and they're being interrogated."

"I hope they can help the police," Honey said faintly. "Somebody needs to pay for this."

♣ ♣ ♣

The chief of police ordered his cars to keep a safe distance of one hundred meters from behind the Lexus filled with hostages until he could speak with the FBI.

Meanwhile, Delano was taking them on a highway chase that would last sixty miles. Inside the vehicle he was chain-smoking the husband's cigarettes.

"Please just let my children go," the woman pleaded. "They're just young girls." The mother's anguish could be heard in her voice. "I know you're a good man. You don't want to do this."

Delano pulled his gat from his waist, and with one arm on the steering wheel, he pointed his pistol at one of the daughters in the back. "Say one more muthafuckin' thing!"

"OK, OK, I'm sorry," she pleaded. "Please don't hurt them."

"You don't know shit about me, bitch! I will put a bullet in your muthafuckin' eye and then stick my dick in it!"

Chief couldn't help but laugh out loud at Delano's foolishness. But he liked his gangsta. He was letting the couple know that they were ruthless and not to be fucked with.

"New rule," Chief joined in. "And I'm only gonna say this once— Get it in your heads that we need quiet time to think straight! We got the whole Las Vegas PD on our asses, so if one of y'all muthafuckas opens your mouth to even sneeze, shorty right here"—He pointed toward the youngest daughter—"gets it! I don't care if you gotta piss. Piss on yourself before you ask some dumb shit like, Can I use the bathroom?"

From that speech Chief knew he'd earned their respect. Now it was time to strategize. "Yo, D, what you thinkin', man? How we gonna lose those muthafuckas?"

Delano shrugged. He looked in his rearview mirror and saw a procession of law enforcement cars keeping a safe distance. "They ain't gonna fall back, man. We need a distraction."

Chief thought quickly and lifted his pistol and blew the father's brains out. Chaos broke out in the mid-sized car as his brains splattered everywhere.

The husband never saw the hit coming. He'd actually been praying to God for a miracle when Chief had decided to improvise. Chief then leaned over, opened the door, and kicked the father's body out on the hot pavement. His body bounced a few times and then came to a complete stop, creating a massive collision as each police vehicle tried to avoid running over him.

"One down, three more to go, if y'all don't stop yelling in my ear!" Chief said.

The daughters hugged each other tight, wishing that this was all a dream.

Delano cut his eyes at the mother. Her body was trembling so violently, it looked like she was going into convulsions. Delano no longer saw the police vehicles following in close proximity, but the helicopters were still hovering. This encouraged him to speed up and really fight to make a getaway. He began weaving in and out of traffic at an unsafe, erratic speed.

"Yo, D, get off this muthafuckin' highway. Go into the hood where those muthafuckin' helicopters can't go!"

"Whatchu mean, Chief? Ain't no restrictions in the hood. What's stopping them pilots from following us? Ain't no stop signs in the sky!"

"Nigga, just do it!"

With nothing to lose and freedom to gain, realizing they were still being followed, Delano found the nearest exit and headed down the ramp. He didn't know how the day would end, but he knew that he wasn't going down without a fight.

Chapter 11

The police precinct was deluged with calls regarding the morning's events. Sergeant David Aponte and first-grade Detective Hernandez had the task of interviewing the two witnesses, while the FBI used one of their conference rooms to look at the video footage from both heists. Never in Las Vegas history had two heists of this magnitude ever been attempted on the same day. The task force was ready to turn the whole zip code upside down if they had to.

"Do you think it's just a coincidence?" Hernandez asked his boss. "Or could they be the same crew?"

"Right now there's no need to speculate. Let's gather facts first and see where that takes us."

Hernandez nodded, although he didn't agree. He loved speculation. He could "conspiracy theory" a situation all day and night; it kept his mind sharp.

The officers decided to question Rosie first, in tandem. They could tell that she was still shaken up.

"Would you like some water? Soda? Could we get you anything?" Aponte asked.

"A soda would be nice," she said weakly. "A Diet Pepsi."

Both officers looked at the overweight Rosie.

"Sure. Detective Hernandez, could you go and get Ms. Rosie a soda."

Rosie cleared her throat. "And I am a little hungry. All this violence has given me an appetite."

Detective Hernandez was slightly annoyed but said nothing.

"What would you like to eat? Would a sandwich be OK? Turkey and cheese or something like that?" Sergeant Aponte asked.

"Didn't we pass by that Mexican restaurant on our way here? I heard their food is really good. Do you think they deliver?" Rosie suddenly found her voice. Quickly she realized that they had to kiss her ass. They needed her. Usually when her ex-husband or brothers were locked up and she walked into a precinct, she was treated like shit. Now that the shoe was on the other foot, she was going to demand respect.

"Sure. We could do Mexican for you. Anything specific?"

"*Al rosso con pollo* with rice and bean, plantains, and salad. Make sure you ask for a double serving of chicken. These restaurants give you two small chicken legs that ain't enough for a small child," Rosie stated. "And don't forget the plantains. I hate when they forget to add the plantains, don't you?"

No one replied.

"I'll have that with the—"

"*Diet* Pepsi," Hernandez interjected. "Anything else? Would you like a few cakes or a couple pies?"

Rosie couldn't tell if he was being sarcastic. "Well, a dessert would be nice, but I don't want to trouble you."

Hernandez smirked.

"It's no trouble at all," Sergeant Aponte added.

While Hernandez was fetching her food, Sergeant Aponte went over the preliminaries and was just about to get into the nitty-gritty when Hernandez came back with the food.

The aroma of the food had Rosie salivating. "I know y'all don't think I can sit here and answer questions with my food just inches from me. I gotta eat now. I ain't going nowhere. Y'all can finish asking questions once I'm done."

Aponte and Hernandez excused themselves from the room while Rosie ate, but they watched her from the other room on video camera.

"I feel like shoving my foot down her greedy-ass throat!" Hernandez stated.

Aponte laughed. "Look at how she's gobbling down those chicken bones. I'd hate to stand between her and a meal. Boy, oh boy!"

"We got three dead security guards and no leads, and her first thoughts are of food," Hernandez remarked dryly. "Should we go and question the other witness?"

"Nah, I sent Wells, Anniston and Agent Peterson in with her. Hopefully they're making more progress."

♣ ♣ ♣

"Go over the story one more time, Ms. Jasmine, just so we could make sure we understand fully," officer Wells asked. His tone was soft and encouraging.

"OK," she said, and exhaled. She was now frustrated. She'd told them the story a million times.

"I get off the bus at approximately eight a.m. as I always do and begin to make my way to the casino. It's a long walk in the summer heat, so I take my time. I get to the back entrance of the Bellagio, and at first, nothing is out of the ordinary. I see the armored car, and then I heard a gunshot. It was loud. I look up, and I see a guy with a helmet and a gun. Immediately, I spin around and run for my life."

"Describe the guy again." Agent Peterson asked.

"He's tall and with average weight. I can't see his face because of the helmet—"

"What race?"

"I don't know. I can't tell. He's wearing gloves. All I remember is that he had a big black gun, and that's all I see."

"So if you can't see his face, how do you know it was a guy?" Wells wasn't really sure why he asked the question, or what he was getting at.

"It was a guy. I just know. The way he moved was like a guy."

Officer Anniston followed up with, "And how many were with him?"

"As I said earlier, I only see him. In my neighborhood you learn that when you hear a gunshot, you run first or you die. I turned around and ran."

"When you say tall, like how tall? Six feet? Taller?"

Jasmine thought about how her eyes scanned up when she heard the shot. The assailant was standing on the loading dock. "I dunno. Maybe six feet. He was standing on the loading dock."

"Is that the reason he looked tall?" Peterson asked, pressing her for answers.

Jasmine couldn't figure it out. Her head hurt. All she wanted to do was go home and be thankful she was alive. The detectives and agent wanted her to solve math equations, have X-ray vision to see through helmets, and also do their jobs. Las Vegas should have tighter security with all this money at stake.

She guessed, "Yeah, at least six-three."

"Yeah, he looked six-three because he was standing on the loading dock, or yeah, he was six-three?"

Jasmine didn't like his tone. She now felt he thought he was better than her. Since he wanted to be a prick, she'd give him a story he'd never forget.

"Yeah, he was six-three. And you know what? I'm remembering more now. I guess I was in shock when you first brought me in, with all the commotion. But he did lift up his helmet for a second, and he was white." Jasmine sat up straight in her seat. "I could see his eyes and nose."

Peterson's smile broadened. "Anniston, go and get the police sketch artist. We might be on to something."

♣ ♣ ♣

When Hernandez and Aponte walked back into the room, Rosie was still licking the food from her fingers. Aponte cleared his throat, which helped the woman focus on the reason she was there.

"Is there anything identifiable that you could tell us about the assailants that would be useful?" Aponte asked. "Did anyone stand out? Could you tell us the race, gender, height, weight, anything you could think of?"

Rosie thought for a moment, "There was one of them, perhaps the ringleader, who I swear I've seen before."

Chapter 12

Luther made his way over to the safe house, according to plan. The room was somber and each girl held a long face. He could hear the faint moans of Tee-Tee, fully in agonizing pain. Blythe tried to comfort her as best as she could but there wasn't much she could do for her friend.

The girls had laid Tee-Tee on a foldaway table that was now saturated with blood. Blythe held her hand tightly, to reassure her friend that she would be OK.

"I'm gonna make it right, Blythe?" Tee-Tee asked.

"Of course, you are. Just as soon as Honey gets here, she'll know what to do." Blythe hated lying to her friend. But what else could she say? It's over for you? You're going to die because we can't take you to a hospital?

"OK," she said, her eyes darting nervously around the room, anticipating that Honey would walk in any second.

"Honey is OK, right, Luther? She made it back safely?"

"She's good. I'm sure she's fine, but we don't have much time. We have to finish part three." He looked at each girl. They looked defeated. He knew he had to take control. "Blythe, give Tee-Tee this. It'll help her with the pain."

Luther tossed Blythe a paper bag with a strong sedative and bottled water. He needed the young girl to be put out of her misery. No need for her to linger around, suffering. Blythe knew that whatever was in the paper bag wasn't a pain reliever, but she gave it to her friend anyway.

She couldn't bear to see her in such agony.

Willingly Tee-Tee swallowed the pills. "Promise me you'll never forget me," Tee-Tee said, her eyes getting heavy.

"What you talkin' 'bout? You're my best friend. Next week we'll be spending all this money together. Far away from here, just like we planned."

Tee-Tee's grip loosened, and her eyes fully closed. Blythe just stared down at her friend and shook her head in disbelief. Tears streamed down her eyes that she quickly wiped away. Everyone was frozen waiting to see how Blythe would react.

"We have to keep moving and finish what we started. Tee-Tee would want that. She was a true hustler."

"I was listening to the radio on my way over here to see if we were hot, and I heard there was another heist done this morning at Harrah's. They got helicopters and FBI on their tails. They done. Ain't no escaping that there," Party said.

Everyone was oblivious that the felons she was referring to not only was connected to Honey by blood, but also were their decoys. Had it not been for their attempted heist, Honey's crew could have never made such a clean getaway.

Luther opened up the back of the minivan and began to count out each bag and then tally up each person's cut.

An hour later, he said, "With the take divided seven ways—"

"Six," Blythe interjected.

"Tee-Tee still gets a cut, Blythe. That's how we do things, and I'm sure that's how Honey would want it. If you could make sure her family gets—"

"She has no family. Not anyone that ever gave a fuck about her. I'm her only family, as she was mine." Blythe's voice cracked at the realization of her friend's passing.

"Then you get her share." Luther exhaled. "With the take divided seven ways, we all walk away with six point three million dollars of unmarked money."

There was a thunderous roar of emotion as the whole room erupted.

Finally, Party spoke, "Dang! We could have had more if we had time to remove all the bags from the truck."

Luther was disappointed with her lack of wisdom, and greed. "Are you stupid, or stupid? If everyone thought like you, there'd be more than one dead girl."

Party lowered her eyes. "Sorry," she said. "That didn't come out as planned."

The massive warehouse held five untraceable used cars. Tee-Tee and Blythe were to ride away in one, and Luther, Party, Mercedes, and Cinnamon would each take one. Each person loaded their cash into the back of their trunks and had less than an hour to get out of Nevada before the police put up roadblocks and began checking identification and the trunks of people's cars. Everyone was headed out except Honey, who needed to remain in Vegas until the heat died down.

Luther thought he heard someone coming. "What's that?"

Everyone began running to pick back up their pistols in anticipation of a raid, until they heard a familiar voice.

"I'm coming in," Honey stated.

Everyone was relieved.

Honey walked in and ran directly toward Tee-Tee.

Before Honey made it to the table, Blythe said, "She didn't make it, Honey."

Honey stopped in her tracks and sighed. "Is everyone else OK?"

"Yeah, we all straight," Party said. "But what are you doing here?"

"I figured as much, but they closed down the casino due to the fact that it's a crime scene, and said we'd all begin getting calls this week to go into the precinct."

"How do you feel about that?" Mercedes asked.

"I'm rock-solid, Mercedes. You know how this goes; the first 48—the heat gets hot. The only thing that's happened that wasn't part of the plan was Tee-Tee getting hit. I told y'all I'd have to go to the precinct."

"Another thing that wasn't part of the plan was the security guard. What about that? You knew him, didn't you?"

"He was a casualty of war. Collateral damage."

"Well, you could have told me. I froze up. What if he hadda put a bullet in my head?"

"What the fuck is your problem?" Honey approached Mercedes. "I did what I had to do to keep the plan running smoothly. This heist was on a need-to-know basis. You didn't need to know shit about that guard."

Mercedes didn't know why she'd just blown her top. Because of Honey she had nearly seven million dollars to spend. And what about how Honey held her down at the heist and made sure she got out of there before the bullets began flying? Mercedes realized she was dead wrong for trying to pick a fight.

"I'm sorry, Honey. I guess I'm still pumped up off adrenalin and still a little scared."

"It's all good." Honey nodded. "I just want y'all to know that I'm proud of each and every one of you. Everyone kept their heads under extreme circumstances. And please note that whatever I kept from anyone of you was for your own good, and it was part of the plan. Had I exposed too much, we all might not be standing here."

"So I guess that means that you're not going to tell us why you had me take pictures of Mercedes and her two kids duct taped?" Party really didn't care. She was all about the bottom line. And her bottom line was almost seven million. But if Honey wanted to spill the beans, she'd listen.

"Exactly. I'm not gonna tell you. Just note that it played an intricate part of us getting away with this heist." Honey ran her hands through her hair and exhaled. "I just want to go over a few more details before we torch this place. Remember what I told y'all. Once you get settled, divide and hide your money in several areas, from bank safety deposit boxes to buried treasures in your private backyards. Never choose a bank that's attached to a mall or next door to a store. Always find a stand-alone bank. Thieves always choose to rob the safe deposit box of a bank that's attached to another unit. It's easier for them to drill straight through. Also, once your money is secure, never, ever transport more than nine thousand dollars at once. Any currency ten thousand dollars or over, the IRS needs to be notified, and the feds could get called in. And don't be a smart-ass and transport nine thousand nine hundred and ninety-nine dollars. When you get settled, find a part-time job."

A few girls grunted.

"I'm telling y'all to heed these words. Find a job in a Starbucks or something where you put in twenty-one hours a week and get medical insurance. Keep those checks going direct deposit into your accounts and use your heist money to pay modest bills. Always buy money orders but not always from the same place. And you can only buy up to three thousand dollars worth of money orders at one time. Anything more than that and guess what? You have to fill out a form for the IRS. Put a down payment on a modest house—not more than nine thousand dollars—and pay your mortgage each month with a money order. And last, don't go buying extravagant cars, no matter how tempted you get. It's not worth it. You don't need a Bentley to make you feel good about yourself. You have almost seven million dollars. That should keep a smile on y'all faces for the next fifty years if you budget it correctly."

Everyone promised that they wouldn't fuck up.

As each girl hopped in their ride, one by one, they all gave Honey a big squeeze.

"Mercedes, don't forget I'm going to contact you in a few days on the throwaway cell phone to make that transaction we discussed. Make sure you hack in on a secure, untraceable Gateway."

"Honey, you can count on me. I was born to ride and override systems and passwords. Whatever you need, consider it done."

"Thanks, babe."

Honey and Luther were left to clean up the mess and cover everyone's tracks. They torched the warehouse with Tee-Tee and all the other evidence, including the FedEx minivan.

"Well, I guess that concludes part three of our plan."

"Isn't that the last chapter?" Luther asked.

"Not at all." Honey smiled. "Not even close."

Chapter 13

Luther was supposed to be our fuckin' decoy—"

"What the fuck happened to him and Cinnamon? You think Honey had something to do with this shit? You think she told them you smoked Meech?"

Chief refused to take the blame for shit going sour. "This ain't got shit to do with Big Meech. That bitch set us up!"

"But why? And, if so, Luther and Cinnamon had to be down. So why would they all turn on us? It doesn't make any sense."

"How you asking me to make it make sense? Nigga, I'm fucked up just like you."

Delano and Chief had driven the hostages into an abandoned used car lot and was held up in an empty office close to the Arizona border. They had run out of gas. The place was surrounded with law enforcement, and the feds had officially taken over the case. The small town was now buzzing with drama. No doubt this heist would put the small town on the map.

The head of the Nevada division, Special Agent Randall Scully, who was in charge of hostage negotiation got on the loudspeaker attached to the local police car. They still didn't have any intel on who the robbery suspects were. They'd lifted so many prints this morning and were still processing names. And although they gave the news media a grainy picture of both suspects, none of the calls from the tip line had garnered any hits, leading them to believe that the suspects were from out of state.

"This is Special Agent Scully. I'm going to toss a telephone inside so

I could speak to the man in charge. I'm going to walk, unarmed, about twenty yards in and then toss the phone. Would that be OK?"

Chief smirked. He crawled to the window and yelled, "Hell muthafuckin' no! That ain't OK. You tryin' to set us up with some sort of explosives! You toss anything and, before it hits the ground, I'll splatter each one of these hostages' brains out before we take our own lives!"

Delano looked at Chief.

"I'm just fuckin' with them. We ain't gonna kill ourselves. Hell muthafuckin' no! I'm a Christian. The only way I'm leaving here is blazing!"

♣ ♣ ♣

Meanwhile, back in Las Vegas, FBI agents were still reviewing the footage from both heists. The second heist from the Bellagio was what intrigued them most.

"Do you think it just started out as a robbery?" one agent commented. "Because we all know robberies tend to turn bad."

"No way! Look at this one. Boom! He takes down the armored guard without provocation. This was premeditated murder. The goal was robbery *and* murder. Look at how he moves," Peterson commented, getting animated. "He's the ringleader. He doesn't hesitate to put a bullet into the guard's head when the other guy hesitates. He's a cold-blooded muthafucka."

"Do you think these are men?" another agent asked. "They're all so tiny."

"One of the witnesses swears she saw the face of the ringleader," Peterson added. "She's confirmed white male. And look at the size of this guy's feet. Agent Scott, zoom in on that guy there who got the drop on the driver."

Agent Scott zeroed in on the Chuck Taylor sneakers. "What size would you say that is? At least an eleven in male. A ten or eleven."

"We'll need to send this footage to NASA and have them give us the accurate height and weight of each suspect. Also, having the correct shoe size will be the cherry on top."

The room soaked in the intel.

"Mexicans. They have to be a Mexican gang." Agent Peterson got excited. "Agent Scott, get on the phone with headquarters and see if they could send us any information state or federal on Mexican perps in the area with a hard-on for robberies of this magnitude. Anyone with a background in bank heists, or snatch-and-grab type of robberies. Anyone that could fit this MO."

"So you're thinking that the two heists aren't related, since the other perps are two black males?"

"I know for a fact that the two aren't related." Agent Peterson continued to study the footage. "This isn't a typical heist by any stretch of the imagination. This crew here has a level of sophistication that isn't present with the two black perps. Their heist was planned to the very last detail. The two from Harrah's are low-level punks who probably took all of a day to plan their heist. That's why they're cornered in a used car lot, and this other group is probably on their way out the country."

The police sketch artist had drawn the face of a white or Hispanic male with a black helmet, the goggles lifted up. His hair color and shape of mouth were unknown. This would be given to the federal agent in charge for the pending press release at eleven o'clock.

"Agent Peterson?"

"Yes."

"We have a dead male found burned at the Super 8 Motel off South Koval Lane," Detective Hernandez stated. His supervisor, Aponte, thought it could be related and wanted to share as much information as possible with the feds. "The motel was set on fire early this morning."

"So?"

Hernandez didn't like his tone. "So, this could be related to the two heists pulled—"

"Thank you, Detective. We're working on our own leads and don't want to be disturbed with innuendo. *Adiós*, Hernandez."

"Innuendo?" Hernandez asked.

"Yes, *innuendo*. That means *speculation*." Agent Peterson felt like he had a hot lead on the Mexican gang and didn't need to be constantly interrupted by Las Vegas PD.

"I know what the fuck it means, asshole!"

Peterson looked up. "You still here?"

Hernandez was boiling with rage. He wanted to punch the daylights out of Peterson. Instead, he stormed out. Peterson couldn't help himself.

"Was it something I said?"

The whole room erupted in laughter.

Luther refused to get out of town as planned. He felt he needed to stick around for a few weeks just to make sure his daughter was cleared.

"You don't have to stay, Luther. You can leave now and start your life over."

"I know what I *can* do, and I also know what I *will* do." He'd made his decision, and it was final. He followed Honey to the Extra Space Storage unit where they'd stored the used vehicle with all their cash in the trunk. That unit held close to fourteen million dollars, and the only thing that kept it secure was a six-dollar lock.

Honey drove the car into the unit, locked it, and didn't look back. It was nearly five in the evening when her and Luther arrived home. Immediately they clicked on the news.

"Police say that they are baffled by two early-morning heists that left seven dead and nineteen injured. I'm standing at the back entrance of the Bellagio Hotel and Casino, where three armored car guards were executed as they dropped off millions of dollars of unmarked cash. Police say a band of thieves descended onto the property and didn't intend on leaving any witnesses. The gang apparently used high-end motorcycles as their getaway, but police aren't saying what form of transportation was used to carry away the money stolen from the heist.

"Later tonight someone from the FBI will be making a statement, but right now they've released this police sketch of one of the ringleaders based on the description given to them by an unnamed witness. The gang is thought to be white male or Hispanic, possibly a Mexican gang. If anyone has any leads, we encourage you to contact the tip hotline. You can remain anonymous. Cathy, now to you over at Harrah's."

Honey looked at Luther.

"This is even better than I'd planned. We're Mexican gang members. Really?"

"Don't get too happy, Honey. They could be blowing smoke up our asses."

Honey shook her head emphatically. "The Bureau withholds evidence. They don't manufacture it to this degree. Notice they never mentioned how much money was stolen. That's done purposely. If they said Mexican gang members, then for some reason that's the intel they've received. I know how these guys work. I was once on the inside, remember? This heist was brazen, and they're going to get a lot of pressure to solve it. Right now their best bet is to get as much information out to the public in order to get any possible leads."

Luther hoped that his daughter was correct. He needed to believe they were in the clear, but his gut kept telling him that it was too easy. And when things were too calm, a storm was always lurking around the corner.

They continued to watch.

"I'm Cathy Hawn over at the gruesome scene this morning when two armed gunmen walked into Harrah's Hotel and Casino brandishing automatic weapons. The head of security, Javier Martinez, was shot and killed on the scene, and several of his men were wounded. The gunmen then took four hostages, the Jolie family, who we're told were here on vacation. The father was brutally shot and tossed out the car on Interstate 15. Right now we have live footage of the two assailants, who are surrounded by Las Vegas police, SWAT, and the FBI. We're told that the assailants are refusing to speak with the hostage negotiator."

Honey and Luther watched as they replayed and earlier footage from the helicopter. It showed a wide shot of the used car dealership and you saw the full magnitude of how the place was heavily littered with law enforcement. Next, it jumped to ground footage in real time and the area had been cordoned off from local pedestrians.

"You had all this planned, didn't you?" Luther asked. "I should have known when you told me that you didn't want me to be a distraction for Chief that it wasn't because you were protecting me. You had other plans, didn't you?"

"Somebody had to take the rap." Honey kicked off her heels.

"And you couldn't think of anyone else to take the fall?"

Honey shook her head. "Sometimes, for the greater good, you gotta do foul things when you're the boss of your crew. Chief wasn't shit, and he never was gonna be shit. He would have blown all that money in days and, in the process, got us all hot. He was in Vegas for less than a month and jeopardized our operation how many times? The prostitute. Big Meech? He was a time bomb just waiting to explode. I just made it so that he would explode in Harrah's Casino."

"And what about the girls? What if they fuck up and get us hot?"

"The women I chose are thoroughbreds and trustworthy."

"Right now they are. You know yourself that the feds won't stop until they nail someone for the Bellagio job."

Honey fixed herself a drink and didn't fix one for Luther. He didn't care. For once in his life he didn't have the urge.

"And they will nail someone for the Bellagio. I've made sure of that."

"Chief. You decided to make Chief the patsy."

Honey took a large gulp of the champagne. "Chief was the decoy—"

"The decoy?"

"Yes, the decoy. He played his part well." Honey took another gulp. She needed to take the edge off her nerves. "There are four parts to a heist."

"Four parts?" Luther repeated. "Since when? All you've run around here preaching is there are three parts to a heist."

"You know I used to think I got my brains from you." Honey laughed playfully. "I guess I gotta officially give Mommy all the credit. As I just said, there are four parts to a heist—the mastermind, the crime, the decoy, and the patsy."

Luther drank in his daughter's words, "And this patsy, you've already chosen him?"

"Them. I've already chosen them."

Luther was relieved that he wasn't the chosen one. He also didn't have any idea who the 'them' were and he realized he didn't care. "Fuck 'em," he replied dryly, and they continued to look on.

♣ ♣ ♣

Somehow Honey had convinced herself that Chief was getting everything he deserved. From being the one to introduce her husband to Olivia and knowing all along that he was fucking her in Honey's house to never crying two tears in a bucket when their mother committed suicide. In her mind, it was all Chief's fault. His constant bungling of his crimes kept their mother's nerves frayed. She'd never forget when she lost her job she went to her brother to help her pay for their mother's therapy because she'd given all her money to the lawyer to defend her against the attempted murder accusation.

"I said I ain't got no paper to waste on this bullshit," he complained. "Mommy need to go ahead and put herself outta her misery. I'm tired of all this soap opera Hollywood drama with her. What black woman you know needs therapy? We were dragged over here on slave ships and now look at us. We eatin' good and drinkin' good," he preached. "Why is everything with her doomsday?! Each day I gotta look at her face all long and twisted up. If she don't like it here she should check the fuck out."

The very next day their mother committed suicide. She had heard what Chief said and felt that they'd all be better off with her dead. Her mother's death had festered in Honey's heart to the point that when she began strategizing the heist, she didn't lose any sleep on her plans for her brother's demise. As much soap opera drama he'd put the family through, he had the nerve to pass judgment.

♣ ♣ ♣

Chief pulled out his spliff that he thought he'd smoke earlier today in celebration. How quickly those tables had turned. The weed, dipped in embalming fluid, and bought from a guy who worked in his father's funeral home, was just what he needed. The putrid smell almost choked his hostages to death. They all began coughing violently but knew better than to object.

As Chief and Delano kept their pistols locked on the hostages, the mother kept her eyes locked on Chief. She wanted to rip him to shreds with her bare hands for the way he was treating them and especially how he brutally murdered her husband.

Chief inhaled the smoke into his lungs and then slowly released. "You got big eyes. A bitch could get killed for eyes like yours."

Instantly, the mother lowered her glare.

Chief passed the spliff to Delano, who inhaled heartily. He hated to think about the inevitable, so instead he focused on how they'd gotten there.

"I'm tellin' you, son, they set us up."

Chief was in a zone. "True. True." He nodded his head, but he was only half-listening. He wondered, if he made the two girls strip, could he get it up? Would the white teenagers have some good pussy or at least know how to suck dick?

"I knew when I walked outside that it was a setup!" Delano began pacing up and down the small office. "I shoulda taken my narrow ass back up North. Now look at my dumb ass."

That snapped Chief out of his zone. "Yo, what the fuck you sayin'? You shoulda left me with my dick in my hands to do this bid by myself?"

Delano put more bass in his voice. "I'm saying that we got set the fuck up!"

Chief shrugged. "Don't make sense."

"What?" Delano screamed, spit flying out of his mouth. "What part of the plan is this? Huh? Because in all the times we went over the plan, I don't remember the part about our getaway vehicle not being outside. And Luther? He wasn't fuckin' there either! That was part of the plan, muthafucka?"

"Calm down, a'ight. A nigga feelin' nice. I need to digest this information and see how the fuck we gonna get up outta here. In fact, order room service. A nigga got the munchies."

Delano wanted to knock Chief's block off for being so cavalier about their situation but he was hungry too. "Yo, these hostages and us captors are hungry up in here!" Delano screamed out the window. "We want a couple pizza pies, some sodas—"

"Make sure you get some Twinkies and salt and vinegar potato chips," Chief told him.

"And we want some Twinkies and potato chips!" Delano shouted.

"Salt and vinegar, D. Damn, this shit is free. Make sure they get it right. This could be our last meal," Chief said in a joke, but no one found it funny.

Delano thought for a moment. "Salt and vinegar chips and Doritos. Y'all got that?"

Agent Scully answered, "Yes, we'll get on this right away, but we'll need something from you. You know how this works—we give you something, you give us something. We want one of the hostages. Send out one of the girls."

Delano didn't even have to think. "Over some potato chips? Get the fuck outta here! Man, suck my dick! These bitches in here hungry! Either send them some food, or one of them will eat a bullet! You got one hour!"

Chief was respecting Delano's gangsta.

Agent Scully had tried. He placed the food order just as it was told as SWAT prepared to position themselves to take out the two young punks.

♣ ♣ ♣

"Yo, I see this nigga dressed in black sneaking around out there, Chief. I'm telling you that's SWAT. Those muthafuckas preparing to take us out."

"They ain't gonna do no shit like that. They can't start blazing with hostages. That's against the law."

"Which law is that? Why don't you recite the CPLR you learned in law school? Please enlighten us, because any second they're about to put our fuckin' lights out!"

Delano began walking toward the window. "Whoever is in charge, I want y'all to send in a telephone like you suggested. I got some shit I wanna say!"

"Delano, man, whatchu doing?" Chief asked.

"I ain't going out without taking that bitch down with us. I don't know why, but she set us up. They need to know she was the mastermind behind all this shit here. If it wasn't for her, we wouldn't even be in Vegas."

"You don't know that for sure, Delano. You just amped right now. Why don't you sit your jumpy ass down."

"Damn right, I'm amped! Our fuckin' heads are on the chopping block."

Chief could see Agent Scully walking toward them with a cell phone in his hand, his arms stretched high in the air in surrender.

"Delano, I ain't no snitch. That shit ain't ever acceptable, no matter what."

"Don't talk to me about what's acceptable. You just killed your man! This is partly your fault. In fact, it's all your fault. If it wasn't for you, me and Big Meech would still be in Harlem huggin' the block. If I go down, so does she."

Chief couldn't explain why snitching on Honey didn't sit too well with him. What if she was innocent? What if something happened, and she was kidnapped, shot, or murdered? What if Javier's goons found her and snatched up Cinnamon and Luther? What if the whole crew was dead? All that could be possible, so to Chief, what Delano was planning on doing was foul. And for what? Chief knew they weren't walking out of there alive, unless they wanted to spend the rest of their lives in a 6 x 6 jail cell.

Chief casually walked up and put one bullet in the back of Delano's head. Before his body could hit the ground, a second bullet followed. Only, that bullet entered the back of Chief's head.

♣ ♣ ♣

"We've got breaking news from the scene of a hostage standoff. Both suspects were taken down. We don't have all the details yet, but we're reporting that both suspects were put down. They're dead. We're told the hostages are all OK. Mother and her two daughters are OK! You can see them in the distance being loaded into the waiting ambulance. We'll continue to update you as more information comes in."

It was only eleven p.m., but Luther had dozed off on the sofa. It was a long, stressful day. Honey wished she could have been asleep as well. She'd partly wished that Chief would have given himself up, but she knew there wasn't any way he would have willingly done any jail time. He'd always said he wasn't built for that lifestyle.

So far, everything was going according to plan—except her heart. She didn't anticipate feeling remorseful about her brother's murder. Was Luther correct? She could have found a different decoy. While planning the heist she thought it was a necessity to kill a few birds with one stone.

As she wrestled with guilt, she drifted off into a violent sleep, only to be awaken hours later drenched in sweat.

It was seven a.m. She called her boss as everyone was told to do. "Hi, this is Honey."

"Honey, the casino is still closed, so no work today. The feds said that we should all be back to work in two or three days."

"That's good. I look forward to a full paycheck, and now I'll have to cut back this month."

"Don't you have any sick or vacation time?"

"Yeah. I could use that?"

"I don't see why not. Especially under these circumstances. I'm contacting the union this morning, but I'm almost certain everyone will get compensated." He coughed violently. "Excuse me. Anyway, I got an e-mail yesterday, and you're on the list to go into the precinct tomorrow to tell what you saw."

"What I saw?" Honey tried to sound disinterested. "I didn't see anything."

"Doesn't matter. It's mandatory. They've compiled the list alphabetically, so you're in the first batch. Is there a problem?"

"Not at all. But would I rather be at a salt-water pool drinking a cocktail on my day off? Most certainly."

He laughed. "I hear ya, doll. And I'd love to see you in that bikini."

"Don't say it!" Honey joked. "Don't do it."

He chuckled. "OK, Honey. I'll see you in a couple days. Don't get too comfortable with your time off."

"I promise I will. Bye."

"Bye, doll."

Honey made herself a cup of coffee and began to mentally prepare for tomorrow's interrogation.

When her father woke up, she told him about Chief, and he just nodded.

"You'll need to contact Aunt Bunny and tell her what happened to Chief. Have her make arrangements to get his body sent back to East Harlem."

"You sure that when the police start digging for relatives that your name won't come up?"

"I'm positive. Honey Atkinson will come up. Chief always listed me under his father's last name since Mommy remarried. Only, I never used it. All my paperwork says either Brown or Robertson, my married name."

"Good. I'll see that they send for his body and that he has a proper funeral. He at least deserves that." Luther poured himself a cup of coffee and then added, "He was a good kid."

Honey didn't like that last quip. When was Chief ever a good kid? He was a raving lunatic who wreaked havoc on all those who loved him. Honey shrugged it off. Aren't people supposed to speak fondly of the dead? She deduced that Luther was just playing a role.

Chapter 14

Honey pulled up to the Las Vegas Police Department headquarters at her scheduled time of noon. She walked to the front desk. "Hi, my name is Honey Brown. I have a noon appointment with Detective Hernandez."

"Have a seat. He'll be with you shortly," the female officer said, barely glancing up.

Honey thought that was rude. Immediately, she fell into a sour mood. As she looked around, everything now annoyed her—the loud noises, the law enforcement lingo, the perps being brought in for processing.

Finally, Detective Hernandez appeared. "Ms. Brown?"

"Yes?"

A broad smile and then, "I'm Detective Hernandez."

Honey extended her hand. "Nice to meet you."

"Likewise. Could you follow me."

Honey was led down a long corridor, where she passed blown-up pictures of both crime scenes, and mug shots of Chief, AKA Corey Atkinson, and Delano Jackson taped to the chalkboard. When she saw a picture of the burnt Super 8 Motel, she wondered did they make a connection. Honey was led into a small interrogation room, which Detective Hernandez said was a conference room.

Honey sat down and felt awkward. Why didn't he speak with her in his office? Was she under arrest? Had one of the girls gotten knocked and gave him the 4-1-1? Had Chief snitched?

Breathe, Honey, she thought. *This will all be over shortly. The hard part's done.*

"Ms. or Mrs.?" Detective Hernandez began.

"Ms. Brown, or Honey." Honey knew better than to try and flirt. That would put him on high alert. She kept her face a mask of stone but softened it slightly when appropriate.

"OK, Honey, could you go over Wednesday, the day of the Bellagio heist for me?"

"Sure, no problem. Well, my day started off normal, until I approached the casino. Something just didn't feel right."

Detective Hernandez inched forward in his chair, an indication that Honey had his full interest. "When you say something didn't feel right, was it because you saw something?"

"I'm not sure if I saw anything that could help you. But my father always said, if you want the right answer, all you have to do is ask the right question."

Hernandez chuckled. "He sounds like a smart man."

Honey nodded. "I think so."

"OK, please continue."

"Well, as I was saying, I just had this eerie feeling when I pulled up. Now, as I look back, it must have been something I saw in everyone's face. It was sheer terror."

"What time did you arrive at work?"

"Between eight fifty and eight fifty-five."

"Could you be more specific?"

"You're joking, right?"

"Not at all."

Honey smirked intentionally. She wanted him to feel that she couldn't understand his logic for wanting to be precise, when she knew perfectly well why that was relevant.

"I'm sorry, I can't."

"OK, that's no problem. Continue."

"Well, as soon as I park my car—"

"Where did you park?"

"I parked in the rear and entered through the side door with the other staff."

"Do you always park in the rear?"

"Yes."

"Did you see anything out of the ordinary? Anyone lingering around that seemed out of place? Any new faces?"

"No. It's a mostly restricted area. Each face I saw was known to me. Once inside I heard all the commotion. I saw mobs of people gathered toward the back entrance, and I hate to admit it, but I was being nosy." Honey shrugged like she was a kid caught in the cookie jar. "Aggressively I pushed through the crowd, and that's when"—She started shaking her head like she couldn't go on with the story.

"And that's when you saw the guards murdered?"

Honey nodded her head.

"In the prior weeks, did anyone stand out? We have reason to believe that they'd cased the casino for months . . . even years."

"Stand out? How so?"

"Like coming around a lot, any new faces, perhaps asking questions?"

"Not at the blackjack table that I can remember. Most of the players keep conversation limited. It's not really a talky-talky game, if you understand what I mean."

Hernandez nodded.

"With the counting of the cards, right?" He tried to make a joke, which Honey didn't find funny.

Hernandez was quiet for a moment, and so was Honey.

"Is there anything ironic or anything odd that jumps out at you about the crime? I mean, anything that you can think of, no matter how small or insignificant it may seem."

Honey thought for a moment then slowly shook her head no, looking the detective square in his eyes.

"Well, OK, Honey, that will be all for today. Here's my card. If you could think of anything else, just give me a call."

Honey took the card and was just about to give him an F for his interrogation skills when he said, "If you want to stop by anytime, we could go over the case. I'm sure you're just as interested in helping us find out who murdered those innocent men and took the casino for nearly one hundred million dollars of marked money."

Aha! Honey thought. *You ain't so bad after all.*

Hernandez had done three things. The first was, he extended an invitation to Honey to be kept abreast of the investigation. Anyone heavily involved in a crime would jump at getting firsthand knowledge of any intel the police have. That way, while playing a witness, they will know if they're a suspect. Second, he nearly tripled the real amount of cash taken, so if Honey was involved, she could have slipped up and said, "I heard they only got a little over forty million." And, last, he lied when he said the money was marked.

"Well, you'll certainly be the first person I'd call if I found out anything new, but I don't think I want to hear any horrible details about the crime. I'm still traumatized from seeing three dead bodies. I'm sure you can understand."

"Certainly. I was just offering you a courtesy. With all these ugly mugs we see daily, it would be nice to be graced with the presence of someone as lovely as yourself."

Honey smiled politely but didn't reply.

Hernandez couldn't read Honey. There was something a little too calm about her. Although she didn't go for his traps, that didn't mean she wasn't affiliated with the heist. She was only his fifth interview, so he decided not to include nor exclude her yet. He certainly knew he'd call her back in. One small part of him wondered, was he going to slightly harass her because she was that fine? He knew he had to tread lightly. His wife was a crazy Cuban and had already threatened to cut his dick off a million times if she ever found him cheating. He loved his wife, but he also loved chocolate pussy. The blacker the berry, the sweeter the juices.

♣ ♣ ♣

Finally everyone was called back to work on Monday. If Honey thought it would be routine, she was dead wrong.

"I'm surprised to see you here," Rosie said condescendingly.

"And why is that? I work here."

"I thought you'd be on an extended vacation somewhere in the South of France getting your already dark body tanned."

"Who could afford that?"

Rosie exhaled. "Not me." And she walked away.

Honey didn't know what to make of that bizarre exchange and just shrugged it off.

The next day Rosie was more direct. "You still here?" she asked.

"What the fuck is your problem?" Honey barked. "You're acting like a mental patient."

Not moved by Honey's aggressive behavior, Rosie said, "I just thought that with the hundred million you and your crew stole the other day that you'd be long gone."

Honey swallowed hard.

"Bitch, are you crazy?"

Rosie inched closer to Honey's face and stared her directly in the eyes. "I'll be all the bitches you want me to be, but I ain't crazy! Either you cut me in on the heist, or I'm going to the cops!"

Honey's eyes popped open in pure shock.

"Oh, you ain't got shit to say now, do you?" Not allowing Honey to respond, Rosie continued, "You got twenty-four hours to get me twenty million dollars, or you go down!"

Honey thought, *The nerve of that fat bitch to want twenty mill, and she didn't even do shit. I planned and executed the whole heist and only walked away with just under seven.*

"The money has been deposited into an off-shore Swiss account by my partners. If you want twenty million, it'll take months for us to withdraw that large amount and get it back to the States undetected. It was hell getting it out on Wednesday."

"That's your problem!"

"Well, do you have any suggestions? Because, if you go to the cops, then your fat ass will stay a fat broke-ass bitch!" Honey couldn't help herself. She had to sling a few insults. Just looking at Rosie's extra rows of skin and jiggling cheeks irked her.

"No need to be so nasty," Rosie said and began to retreat. The look in Honey's wild eyes had unnerved her. She remembered all the dead bodies. "Well, if I gave you my account number, would that be easier for you to transfer the money? At least some of it? A few hundred thousand, so I could pay some bills and buy a new car. If you do that within twenty-four hours, then that'll buy you time to get the rest before I go to the cops."

"How do I know you haven't gone already? How do I know you're not wired?" Honey grabbed Rosie by her plump hand. "Let's go!"

"Go where?" Rosie panicked. Did Honey have a gun? Would she shoot her?

"We're taking a trip into the ladies' room."

Rosie was relieved. Once inside the stall and Rosie proved to Honey that she wasn't wired, Honey's voice softened.

"There's more than enough money to go around," Honey said. "All you have to do is keep your mouth shut and don't run to the cops."

"I haven't said a word. I was in there giving them false leads."

"Let me ask you a question. If the police didn't turn you on to me, how did you know?"

Rosie smiled.

"I didn't see much that day, but I did see someone that I thought was a man dressed in all-black with a helmet on."

"So?"

"Well, before I turned to run, this same man adjusted his neck from side to side, just three quick-paced head movements, and it hit me. I've seen you do that same maneuver a million times. Each time you get out of your car in the mornings, you do that same routine. Each time you setup at your blackjack table, you do that same routine. I always wondered why but never asked. And the last dead giveaway was the green bandana on your arm. You always wear something green and it seemed out of place that a robber would choose a green bandana and not red or blue for the bloods or crips."

"That's it?"

"That's all I needed. I knew it was you."

Honey could have slapped her own face. How could she have been so dumb? With all the elaborate planning, she got pinched by a wannabe detective because of some head movements and a green scarf.

"You're one smart lady, Rosie. And I'm sorry about the 'fat' remarks."

"No need to apologize because, once I get that money, guess who will have access to even more food?"

"Good. I'm glad no hard feelings. I'll need your account numbers if you're serious about getting paid."

"Of course, I'm serious. Do you have a pen?"

"I'll need the routing numbers as well."

"No problem." Rosie began digging in her purse for something to write on.

"Do you have your checkbook on you?" Honey casually asked.

Rosie hesitated.

"It would be easier to just have a check. I don't want anything to go wrong with the transfer. The check will have both."

Rosie reached into her purse and pulled off one check. Before handing it to Honey, she wrote VOID in large letters. *You just can't trust anyone*, she thought.

♣ ♣ ♣

From the secure line, Honey called Mercedes.

"Change in plans," she said, and read off the routing and checking account numbers. "Split the money between accounts."

"How are things going in Vegas?" Mercedes asked.

"They going," Honey replied. "Don't worry about me. Things are good. I can hear seagulls and waves crashing, so I know you're good. Take care of yourself, Mercedes. You won't hear from me anytime soon unless it's urgent. Remember that."

"I'll remember." Mercedes was just about to hang up, and blurted. "Honey."

"Yes?"

"It was nice knowing you."

Honey smiled inside, "We'll meet again."

Chapter 15

"Who's that?" Rosie thought she heard something and sat straight up in her bed, listening.

Meow! Pebbles, her cat, hopped on the bed.

Rosie was relieved. She was on high alert and thought she would feel this way until she had the money in her hands. She didn't like the way Honey had looked at her. It was a cold, heartless stare that chilled her bones. And the vision of the bodies on the hot pavement riddled with bullets was frightening.

She wanted a midnight snack to calm her nerves. Groggily, she stumbled into the kitchen.

"Don't turn the light on!"

"Ahhhh!" Rosie screamed.

A strong hand immediately silenced her around her mouth and something firm pressed into her kidney.

"Don't be frightened," Honey said. She was sitting calmly at Rosie's kitchen table. "No one's going to hurt you. Now if I ask my good friend here to take his hand off your mouth, do you promise you won't scream?"

Rosie nodded emphatically.

"Good. Luther, will you do the honors of releasing our new partner in crime."

Slowly Luther dropped his arm.

"W-w-what are you doing here?" she asked weakly, her knees buckling under the stress of the situation.

"Well, earlier I didn't quite tell you the truth about the money," Honey said, her voice level and calm. "It isn't in a Swiss bank account."

"It isn't?"

"No. That type of shit you only see in movies. Where my black ass gonna get a Switzerland connect?"

"I dunno."

"And you don't have to know, because it ain't true. I just said that to buy time, just in case you were setting me up with the cops."

"I told you I didn't go to the cops."

"I know. And I believe you. But my friend here, he doesn't believe you."

Rosie looked into Luther's menacing eyes and then down at his large gun. He never said one word.

"But I'm telling you the truth."

"Here's what you're gonna do for us, Rosie. You're gonna leave town tonight and promise you won't return."

"But where will I go?"

"Rosie, with fifteen million dollars you can go anywhere on this green planet."

"Twenty million," Rosie corrected.

"Rosie, are you really gonna argue with a man holding a gun?" Honey asked. "It was hard enough for me to get him to cut you in. He's not the most reasonable man in the world. Just look at him."

Rosie cut her eyes toward Luther.

"Does he look reasonable to you?"

Rosie shook her head no.

"Correct. Now hurry up because we're running out of time."

"Hurry up for what?"

"Rosie, you have to follow along now. I can't keep repeating myself. You're leaving town, remember?"

"But where's my money?"

"We have to go and get it. Now pack only your necessities."

Rosie was led back into her bedroom, where she loaded up her suitcase with her valuables.

"What about Pebbles?"

Honey looked perplexed. "Oh, your cat?"

"Yes. I can't leave her."

"Then take her too. That's not a problem."

Honey took the driver's seat, with Rosie riding shotgun, Luther crawled in the back, and the three took off.

Seconds before they arrived at the pre-dug grave in the Nevada desert, Rosie began getting suspicious. "What are we doing this far out? I don't suspect there's much of nothing around here." She clasped her chubby hands together to stop them from trembling.

"Nothing much, but fifteen million dollars," Honey remarked. "You didn't think we'd hide it in town, did you?"

"I guess I never thought about it."

"You didn't think about it because you weren't down with the plan. You never had to concern yourself with the details or cry over your friend who caught a bullet for the millions you're trying to get your greedy hands on."

Rosie thought Honey's voice had become edgier. "Now calm down, Honey. If it weren't for me, you'd be in jail right now."

Honey pulled over and shut the lights on the car.

"If it weren't for you, you'd be alive right now. Bitch, get the fuck out the car!" Honey's voice was gruff. "Are you thanking yourself for your own murder?"

Luther was already out the car and at Rosie's side. When he swung the door open, Rosie tried in vain to shut it back. She began pleading, "Honey, you don't have to do this. I promise, I won't tell a soul."

Luther reached in and grabbed a chunk of her stringy hair.

"Ooooooowow!" Rosie screamed as she was dragged out the car. "Pleeeeassse, don't do this!" Rosie fell to her plump knees, crying and begging. Then she said, "I told them! I told the police! If you kill me, you'll go to jail for murder!"

Honey bent down and spat in Rosie's face. "I would love to get knocked for your murder. It would be my pleasure."

That wasn't the response that Rosie wanted or expected to hear. "Honey, please, woman to woman, don't let him do this to me."

"OK, I won't," Honey sang. "Don't worry at all."

"No!" Rosie cried. "You're lying, aren't you?"

Honey wanted her to go to her grave tormented. She thought about all the lives that were sacrificed to pull off this plan with fluidity⊠the prostitute, Big Meech, Chief, Delano, Tee-Tee, Brian, and many more. And for Rosie to come in at the thirteenth hour and demand a cut of that dirty blood money had Honey seeing red. She wanted to hear Rosie begging for her life and also have the satisfaction of taking it away. Luther wasn't going to kill Rosie, she was.

Yelling and screaming, Rosie put up a good fight as Luther tossed her into the pre-dug grave, which was at least six feet deep. Honey and Luther both watched as she tried to claw her way out to no avail. She'd get at least one foot up before ultimately sliding back down, which no doubt frustrated the frantic Rosie. Honey watched as Rosie exasperated herself, while Luther went and got Pebbles.

"Rosie, how many pounds would you say you've lost these past ten minutes?" Honey joked. "Who knew that Honey could do what Jenny Craig can't?"

"Stop it!" Rosie screamed. She couldn't take any more fat jokes. "You're a mean, horrible person, and you're going to hell!"

"You first!" Honey pulled out her pistol and emptied her clip into

Rosie. Her heavy body fell like a sack of potatoes.

"What about her cat?" Luther asked.

"We're not cat killers!" Honey said. "The cat goes with us. We'll find it a good home."

Chapter 16

Honey and Stephon were in Stephon's stretch Hummer, headed to her favorite seafood restaurant. She hated that Stephon drove the huge limo around town even when he wasn't working, because it drew way too much unnecessary attention to them.

"You believe this muthafucka is pulling me over? I know I ain't do shit!" Stephon said with his short-fused temper.

"Baby, just chill. Show them the paperwork and keep it moving."

Stephon who was a bit of a hothead instantly exited the vehicle and started to approach the unmarked police car with his hands up, motioning and asking what had he done and why were they pulling him over.

"Get the fuck up against the car!" the white female detective shouted at him after she exited her car and drew her gun.

The sight of the officer's gun made Stephon think twice. "What did I do?"

The female cop kicked his legs apart and frisked him as Detective Hernandez looked on. "How many passengers are in the car with you?" she asked.

"Just one, my girl. She's in the front seat," Stephon replied while handcuffs were applied to his wrists.

Detective Hernandez made his way to the front passenger door and opened it. "Ms. Brown, can you please step out of the car?"

Honey looked shocked and confused. "Officer Hernandez?" she said. "What's going on?"

Hernandez had a stern look on his face, and wasn't as cordial as when he'd interviewed her at police headquarters the other day. He ignored her and spoke with authority. "Turn around and place your hands behind your back."

"For what?" Honey knew that he had to tell her why he was placing her under arrest.

"Honey, you know this cop?" Stephon was still absolutely clueless about Honey's involvement in the biggest casino robbery in Las Vegas history.

"Baby, it's nothing but some bullshit. I'll explain it to you later," Honey said. "I know my rights, Hernandez, and you need to tell me why you're placing me under arrest."

"We have probable cause to believe that you were involved in the Bellagio robbery." Detective Hernandez placed the handcuffs on her.

"What?" Honey turned and yelled. Instantly her heart began to pound a mile a minute.

Honey wasn't sure what Hernandez knew. Or if someone had snitched. But one thing she was sure of, they had done their homework if they knew who Stephon was. Especially considering that she had spent the past year keeping her personal life a secret. So she knew the cops had been following her, but she just didn't know for how long.

As Honey shook her head and made her way to the unmarked police car, she also wondered had she somehow slipped up. Her mind was racing non-stop. She sat in the back of the car and she knew that more than ever she had to be super strong at that point and she couldn't show any cracks in her armor.

Once Honey was secure inside the back of the police car, the female cop took the handcuffs off Stephon and asked him for his driver's license and registration.

Stephon went into his wallet and handed both pieces of identification to the officer. She examined them really quick but she didn't have to run the information through her computer because they had already done their research on Stephon and they knew that he was clean. The officer handed him back his license and his registration.

"Stephon, the next time an officer pulls you over, you don't exit your car like a raving lunatic! You understand me?" The butch-looking cop barked. She adjusted her bulky bulletproof vest.

Stephon nodded his head once, but it was barely visible to the officer.

"Do you understand me?" she asked again.

"I nodded my head yes! What the fuck more you want from me?"

"Watch your fuckin' tone! I'm trying to save you from getting your fuckin' head blown off, which I was two seconds from doing when you exited the car the way you did. Now you have a nice day. You're free to go," she said. And then her and Hernandez made their way back to their unmarked car.

"Where are you taking my girl?" Stephon asked.

Hernandez turned and told him, "She will have an opportunity to call you later and tell you where she is."

Stephon had no idea what the hell had just happened. He was so far from street life, he had never in his life seen the inside of a police station, so he couldn't make head nor tails of the situation.

"You know this is some bullshit, right? I had lobster tails and fried shrimp calling my name, and here y'all come with this shit," Honey said to the cops as they drove. She fidgeted, trying to get comfortable, which was difficult to do with the handcuffs.

The cops completely "igged" her as they drove, a tactic she was all too familiar with. But she also knew tight handcuffs usually meant that the suspect was guilty and the cops knew it. But if the cuffs weren't that tight, it was usually a sign that the cops didn't have rock-solid evidence. The logic was, Why make the cuffs super tight and piss off a suspect that you need on your side?

When they arrived at the police station, Honey was walked into a different, much larger interrogation room, where Hernandez handcuffed one of her wrists to a chair and then left her alone. Splattered all across a large wall were pictures from multiple crimes—the Bellagio, Harrah's, Super 8 Motel and the warehouse. An old mug shot of her brother, Chief, blown up to an 8 x 10, along with Delano and Big Meech. And multiple pictures of the front, side, and back entrances of both casinos, as well as pictures of the slain individuals. What wasn't shocking but still disturbing was a blown up picture of Tee-Tee. Obviously forensics had pulled her dental records off her charred body and connected her to the Bellagio heist.

Shortly thereafter, Hernandez walked in by himself with a cup of hot coffee and sat down at the table across from Honey. "Ms. Brown, you want anything to eat?" he asked her.

"No, thank you," Honey replied.

"What about to drink? Are you thirsty?"

"No. No, thank you," Honey repeated.

"Honey, when we were here last time I made it clear that I wanted you to give me anything that was odd or that stood out or that was ironic about the crime that you witnessed at the casino, and you drew blanks."

Honey nodded her head in agreement.

"So let me ask you now, is there anything about that crime that you want to tell me?" Honey shook her head no, looking straight at Hernandez as he sipped on his coffee.

Hernandez then reached inside a manila envelope and pulled out three glossy photographs, duplicates of what was taped on the wall, of the armored truck guards who had been killed, including Brian.

"Do any of these three men look familiar?" Hernandez asked.

Honey examined the photos. While she looked at them, she was scrambling her mind, trying to think of how she should handle this.

"Obviously these are the murdered armored truck guards," she said.

Hernandez drank some more of his coffee before he continued to speak. "Correct. Do you know any of them personally?"

"Personally? No."

Hernandez was persistent. He pushed the pictures back toward Honey. "Take another look, Ms. Brown. Are you sure you don't know any of these guards on a personal, let's say, intimate level?"

She pointed toward Brian's picture and stated, "We fucked once, but when I found out he was married, that was a wrap." Honey was emotionless. "As you can see, I moved on."

With her ATF training, Honey knew that for Detective Hernandez to pursue that line of questioning, the cops had to have some sort of intel on her and Brian. How did they find out? Honey had no idea? But she did know that had she lied she would have walked herself off a cliff.

"Oh, so you knew him intimately. Why didn't you tell me that?"

"Like I told you before, if you want answers, all you have to do is ask the right questions. You never asked me if I intimately knew any of the guards," Honey responded.

Detective Hernandez was furious at her response. He wanted to blow his fucking top. Usually, had this been under different circumstances, he would have snatched the perp up by the collar and roughed them up. But he had to tread lightly with this one. He knew going into the interrogation that Honey was no dummy, but he still felt he was smart enough to outfox her. He thought he had the element of surprise and that Honey would've denied knowing Brian.

"Tell me about your relationship with Brian. Things didn't go so well, did they?"

"You tell me how that went. Obviously you've done your due diligence."

"I don't like you," Hernandez replied, after a long stare down.

"Likewise."

"When I slap those silver bracelets on your wrists and charge you with felonious murder, I hope you still have that smug look on your face."

"Am I not being charged with a crime? Yet I was dragged down here? What kind of illegal process is this?" Honey refused to back down. "And how are you questioning me without reading me my rights? Anything I say or said wouldn't be admissible, and you know this. So why are you jeopardizing your case with these weak-ass mind games? Either charge me, or I want a lawyer. Snap! Snap!"

Hernandez glared at Honey. She was right. He was jeopardizing his case.

Something about the Mexican theory just didn't ring true to Hernandez. They'd hit dead lead after dead lead, but the feds were moving full steam ahead. When he got a tip that Honey had had an affair with one of the murdered armored guards, was an employee at the casino, and failed to mention it during her interview, he knew he'd hit pay dirt. He called the assistant district attorney and explained what he'd uncovered, but they didn't bite. They said his evidence was circumstantial and that he'd better keep his distance from Honey. Though he'd agreed verbally, he had every intention of putting her on the hot seat. He wanted his foot on her throat, until she couldn't breathe.

Hernandez hoped that if he let Honey know she was a suspect that eventually the pressure would get to her and she'd begin to overthink things and perhaps make a move that she wouldn't have made under normal circumstances. He couldn't quite place his finger on why he felt so strongly about her involvement, but it had to do with the complexity, precision, and execution of the heist. He knew she was connected. He just didn't know how deep. All he wanted to prove was that Honey and Brian were in collusion together and came up with the master plan to rob the Bellagio, but somehow Brian got double-crossed.

He looked at Honey, and a smirk came across his face. He sipped more of his lukewarm coffee. He knew that 'Brian' was the hot button but he hated the fact that she had just slung the lawyer word.

Finally Hernandez spoke. "OK," he said, and he stood up and exited the room.

"OK, what?" Honey was slightly worried. No one knew about Brian, except Mercedes. Had Mercedes gotten knocked? Had Brian told someone about the heist? *Who the fuck is snitching?* she thought.

An hour later the female cop came into the interrogation room and introduced herself to Honey. "Honey, I'm Detective Lynch."

"And?"

"Hernandez likes to beat around the bush and walk people around the block. But, me, I'm a straight shooter. And we both know that you want to get out of here and go and enjoy that seafood dinner that's waiting on you. So what I need is for you to be straight-up with us so that we can work together at solving this crime and totally eliminating you as a suspect."

"So now I'm a suspect? Unreal." Honey shook her head. "If I'm a suspect, then I'm free to walk the fuck outta here until you officially charge me! Instead, you slam me up against the hood of a car and detain me. So either I'm under arrest, or you can take off these muthafuckin' handcuffs!"

"Honey, let's cut the bullshit. Of course, you're a suspect. You were fuckin' the armored guard who got killed in the heist, and you didn't tell anyone, and you didn't disclose that information to Detective Hernandez."

"Since when does a one-night stand equate to my having my lover killed and the casino robbed? I would say that's a stretch of anyone's imagination."

"Then why did you hide it if it was a trivial fact? We are conducting a high-profile investigation. You should know better than to withhold information that may or may not be relevant to a case. The fact that you weren't honest with us puts you number one on our radar."

Honey looked at Detective Lynch and rolled her eyes. "Listen, your police problems are your problems. It's not my job to solve your investigation. Now, for the umpteenth time, "she screamed, "Either arrest my black ass, or turn me loose!"

Officer Lynch smiled and then said to Honey, "OK, since you want to do this the hard way, you're free to go but you better keep looking over your shoulder because we're coming for you."

Honey held up her middle finger with her free hand.

"OK, fuck me. Cute. But help me with one thing before I turn you loose." Officer Lynch then pulled out a picture of Brian and his family and showed it to her. "You see this young lady right here?" She pointed to the woman in the picture.

Honey was stone-faced and didn't say anything or show any emotion.

"She lost a husband and she has to raise these four young boys on her own. But, more than anything, she needs closure, Honey, and it's closure that only you can provide. I know that things didn't go as planned that day at the heist, and you had your own reasons for taking him out. Tell me, Was he down with the heist? Did he change his mind and want to stop it in progress? Now is your time to get anything off your chest. But Honey, this young lady right here, she needs to know the truth. Come clean about your involvement in his murder. She already knows that you were sleeping with her husband, but she wants to know what her husband's involvement in the Bellagio heist was. When he was murdered, she came to us for answers."

Honey leaned forward and took a close look at the family photo. She wanted to implode when she realized who Brian's wife was. Honey had never seen any pictures of Brian's wife or his kids. But at that moment she realized that she had seen her before. In fact she had beat her down just a couple weeks back. Brian's wife was the dark-skinned bleach-blonde chick who was staring Honey down in the bar.

Fuck! Honey thought to herself.

Honey had no idea when she'd first met Brian that he was a sloppy cheater. His sloppiness had raised his wife's radar right from the beginning of their affair. The only thing Honey didn't know was if Brian had ever told his wife of his plans to knock off the casino.

Honey held her ground. She didn't let Detective Lynch sway her. "He had a very beautiful family, and I wish I could help you. But like I told Detective Hernandez, y'all on some different shit, with detaining me and this interrogation. I'm not saying anything or answering anymore questions until my lawyer gets here."

Detective Lynch had just given the best performance she could give, but Honey wouldn't budge. Right now they didn't even have enough to keep her on a twenty-four-hour hold. Hernandez and Lynch both knew it was a long shot in cracking someone who was involved in such an elaborate and highly sophisticated crime by pulling on her heartstrings. And since they didn't have any real probable cause to hold her, they unclasped the cuffs and told her she was free to walk out of there.

In the corridor of the precinct, much to her surprise, Honey laid eyes on Stephon and an unknown white gentleman. They were speaking to an officer at Intake. When Stephon saw Honey, his eyes lit up. He extended his arms, and she walked into a warm embrace.

"I was so worried about you," he placed a wet kiss on her lips. "The only thing I thought to do was get an attorney."

Honey smiled. "You did the right thing."

"Honey, this is Chip Levine. He's the best there is out here and also one of my clients."

"Ms. Brown, nice to meet you." Chip looked up and saw Detectives Hernandez and Lynch hovering in the background. "Let's talk outside, shall we?"

As Stephon, Chip, and Honey made their way through the police station, an irate widow greeted them.

"Bitch, you was fuckin' my husband, and now he's dead because of you!"

Those words echoed through the quiet police precinct, interrupting the little cipher that Honey, Chip, and Stephon were having.

"Yeah, that's right, bitch. I'm talking to your ass, Honey!"

Finally everyone was able to see a dark-skinned bleach-blonde female emerging from around a bend in the police station and heading straight toward Honey.

Detectives Hernandez and Lynch had purposely allowed Brian's widow to leave their desk at the same time that Honey was being released, simply because they wanted to cause a confrontation, just to rattle Honey. The exact reason why Brian's widow had been called down to the police station.

"Yo, who the fuck is this?" Stephon asked.

Detective Hernandez ran up to Brian's widow and held her back, telling her to calm down.

"No, fuck that! That bitch is the reason my husband is dead, and she just gets to up and leave? This shit ain't right!"

Chip looked perplexed as he ushered Stephon and Honey outside. Honey kept her cool and gave Hernandez an amused look. Not a complete smile, her lips curled just enough so he could see that she knew what he was up to. In return, Hernandez gave her a slight head nod. "You home-wreckin' whore!" the bleach-blonde yelled after them.

Honey so desperately wanted to confront that bitch and beat her ass again but she knew that she had to maintain her cool.

"Yeah, keep ignoring me, but you know what the fuck you did! And you know the guilt is killing you!" she shouted.

Outside Stephon asked again, "Who was that? What's going on? You seeing somebody else?"

Honey shook her head. "Last year when I first got to Vegas, I met someone. He said he was single but was really married. When I found out, I broke it off. That's it. His name was Brian, and he was one of the guards that got murdered at the Bellagio. Simple, end of the story."

"And his grieving wife has implicated you?" Chip knew there had to be more to the story.

"She needs to blame someone, and in her eyes I'm the dirty mistress. I know the feeling. I've been there."

Both Stephon and Chip tried to read Honey, but her answers were short, and her body language relaxed.

"Well, Stephon has my number. If these detectives continue to harass either one of you, just give me a call, and we'll go to the Civilian Complaint Review Board and file a claim."

"Thanks, Chip."

"Anytime, Stephon."

Honey ended up going to Stephon's house, where she spent the night. She was definitely not in the mood for sex because her nerves were shot. And thank God, for her sake, that Stephon didn't push up on her for any, because she didn't want to turn him down.

But as Honey lay in Stephon's bed unable to fall asleep, she had to admit to herself that the bleach-blonde chick was right about something; the guilt killing her. All Honey could think about as she lay there was the picture of Brian and his family that Detective Lynch had shown to her. She knew that, because of her, Brian's family wasn't a family anymore.

Honey was resilient though, and she wasn't about to crack. She knew that dirty money usually came at a high price. And although she was emotionally bleeding, she reasoned that she literally had millions of reasons that would help to ease her guilt. She couldn't wait until the day came when she could start spending those millions.

The Patsy

♥ *Introducing Kim K.* ♥

pat·sy (pts)
n. pl. pat·sies Slang

*1. A person easily taken advantage of,
cheated, blamed, or ridiculed.*

2. a scapegoat

Chapter 17

Olivia drove down 145th Street in her brand-new Maserati, compliments of her new husband, André. She had been fucking him since she was thirteen years old, and after his first marriage she never thought he'd actually marry her. When she found out that he had married Honey, she herself was nine weeks pregnant. She ran and got an abortion. The humiliation was too much to take.

But only a few weeks after he'd tied the knot, he came back around begging and pleading for forgiveness. He swore that he never loved Honey and had made a mistake when he proposed to her.

At first, Olivia played hard-to-get back. There wasn't any way she'd forgive him so easily. Not when his bitch was sporting an 8-carat diamond and platinum ring, not to mention she also had his last name. No, Olivia fancied herself smarter than the average chick. She knew that men liked a challenge and she had been too available for André. This time around, things would be different. When he called, she pressed IGNORE on her cell phone. When he dropped by asking her mother where was she, she instructed her mother to not give up any details.

Meanwhile she was busy giving herself a makeover. She went to the Dominican hairstylist and dyed her dark brown hair red and had it cut into layers. The reddish color highlighted her light skin nicely. And although she'd never admit her next move, she went to the garment district in lower Manhattan in the wee hours of the morning and loaded up on imitation gear. From Seven Jeans to Prada bags, she bought it. She had a good eye for what looked the most authentic, and that's what she focused on. Olivia knew that the trick to pulling off her new merchandise was to mix it with the real McCoy. So when André spotted her in Club Déjà Vu with skintight Seven Jeans, authentic Manolo Blahnik stilettos, and her fake Prada bag, he did a double take. It didn't hurt that a rival drug dealer was all up in her face and they were popping Cristal and Moët.

That night André begged her to leave with him.

"And go where? To a fuckin' hotel?" she yelled. "Get the fuck outta my face!"

"Why you actin' like that?"

"Go home to your wife!" Olivia wanted to scratch his eyes out.

"It ain't even like that."

Two days later she was home when a florist rang her bell with a dozen red roses and a card from André. She was delighted but still refused to call him. She wanted more.

When André spotted her riding shotgun with Hedge, a baller from Brooklyn, she got it. The next delivery was a full-length mink coat. The card read:

If you won't let me keep you warm, only let this coat take my place!

The coat was cute, but she wanted diamonds. She knew that would take a little more than ignoring him. She'd have to start taking his calls.

They met like two thieves in a restaurant in the Bronx. Olivia told André of the humiliation she'd suffered, how she was starting over, and how she wanted to seriously give Hedge a shot.

"Don't do that to me, Olivia. Don't give my pussy away! I swear, I don't love that bitch!"

"But you married her!"

That night at the Marriot Hotel Olivia fucked André like she'd never fucked a nigga before. She rode him until he screamed her name, and when he woke up in the morning she wasn't there.

If he wants to play mind games, then that's exactly what he would get, she thought.

Soon she had André in the palm of her hands. And when she suggested that she no longer wanted to sneak around in hotels, he didn't hesitate to invite her over to his apartment that he shared with his wife, Honey, and even make love to her on the bed he shared with her.

Olivia wanted to fuck on Honey's sheets. She felt more anger toward Honey for causing her pain than she did toward André for inflicting it.

For years, they continued their affair unbeknownst to anyone. And for playing the secondary position, Olivia was rewarded all the gifts his drug money could afford. He lavished her with impromptu shopping sprees, weekend getaways, and diamond trinkets that cost him a few stacks per purchase. But what she wanted most, he was unable to give her, until one fateful night when Honey arrived home earlier than scheduled and caught them making passionate love.

Her and André were so into their lovemaking, neither one of them heard her come in. They fucked from the bedroom, throughout the kitchen, and had made their way to the living room, where they were ultimately busted. They didn't stand a chance against the Glock-carrying Honey.

If Olivia felt humiliated when she'd heard the news of André's first wedding, getting put outside, naked, in below-zero weather was a vision too hard to repress. She still woke up some nights in a cold sweat.

In Olivia's opinion, André, hell-bent on revenge, played himself by going down to the precinct and filing fake charges on his wife. He knew that Honey's job was all she had, and he wanted to take that away from her. It took a year of court appearances before the charges were eventually dropped. From there Honey disappeared, and no one had heard or seen her since.

♥♥♥

Olivia only had a few errands to run before she met with her best friend April for lunch. She was the new owner of a Dominican beauty parlor—Olivia's—two doors down from the famous Willie Burger on 145th. The shop made a minimum of thirty thousand a month, after expenses. André was so happy that he'd listened to her when she kept begging him to open up a shop for her. She didn't work in the shop because she didn't have her cosmetology license, but she did manage it and was there six out of the seven days they were open weekly. She'd hired a slew of bi-lingual Dominican women as beauticians, and her aunt was the manager. It helped that Olivia was half Puerto Rican because Latino women stuck together. They would have never worked for her if she were all African American.

"*Hola,* Evelyn," Olivia said to her aunt and gave her a peck on the cheek. Evelyn was in her fifties with saggy titties, bleach-blonde hair and always wore what most considered "Spanish colors"—hot pink, dark purple, and bright yellow. Her clothes were too tight, too young, and too colorful, but everyone loved her.

She greeted Olivia warmly, and they both walked to the back for Olivia to collect the money to make the deposit. Olivia made sure that, with the kind of money they collected throughout the day, two deposits were done so as to not have money pile up. Although Harlem was known for making money and not taking money, with the looming recession, you could just never be too careful.

"We made four thousand this morning." Evelyn handed Olivia a Chase money sack.

"That's a good look."

"It's super busy today because everyone is getting ready for the Ruckers basketball game this afternoon. Are you going?"

"Yeah, April and I are going to grab something to eat and then head over."

"Is André going to be there?"

"No doubt. One of the teams playing is his. He has forty thousand ridin' on this game."

"His team will win."

"I should hope so, but they say Fat Joe's team is the one to beat."

Evelyn shrugged. "For Fat Joe's sake, his team better lose. I'd hate to see a rapper gunned down over basketball."

Olivia smirked. "André ain't that stupid." What she wanted to say was, "André ain't that smart," after witnessing the dumb shit he'd done throughout the years.

Olivia liked to stand in line at the teller when depositing cash, but today was extremely busy. The bank only had two tellers working, so she decided to go to the drop box. She filled out the slip, inserted her card, and dropped in the envelope. What she didn't expect was the receipt to read: $960,000 as her checking balance, which was $950,000 more than she had in her checking account.

"This can't be right," she said out loud. She needed a second look. While Olivia stood in line, a million things went through it, until finally she went with her gut and walked off.

Seconds later she turned back around and stood in line. She was completely freaked out. Did André deposit almost a million dollars of drug money into their account to launder? Was he that stupid? There wasn't any way that her business could justify that kind of income.

Like clockwork André would deposit nine to fifteen thousand a week, which they would pay taxes on. That was reasonable. But almost a million dollars was ridiculous.

"Welcome to Chase. How may I help you?"

"Could I have a withdrawal slip, please?" Olivia pulled out her bank card and slid it through the card reader. After punching in her security code, she quickly filled out a withdrawal slip for one hundred dollars.

"How would you like the bills?"

"In twenties, please."

Olivia watched the teller's eyes stretch open in shock, and then she readjusted them. "Do you want to take it from your savings or checking?"

"Checking, please."

The teller processed the withdrawal, and Olivia was on her way. Once again she looked down at the receipt and saw nearly a million dollars. She needed to speak with her husband.

After April and Olivia ate brunch at Amy Ruth's restaurant, Olivia sped over to 155th Street and Frederick Douglass Boulevard to Ruckers Park for the Ruckers championship basketball game. André was pissing her off because he refused to pick up for any of her calls. She found him on the court fully engrossed in a pep talk with his team. When Olivia came strutting down the court in the hot summer heat, booty shorts, tank, and stilettos, she could feel each player's gaze. She loved the attention.

André turned to face her, slightly irritated that he was interrupted, yet pleased with her appearance. She definitely was a head-turner.

"You don't know how to pick up your phone?"

He loved her sassiness. "You see I'm out here handling business. I was gonna get right back."

Olivia rolled her eyes. "We need to talk."

"A'ight, hold up." He turned his back on her and faced his team.

"Now." Olivia aggressively pulled him by his arm. "Excuse me, fellas, this will only take a few minutes."

André allowed himself to be led away. "What is it that's so important that it's coming in between me and my forty stacks?"

"Yo, did you put any money into our account?"

André nodded.

"Where the fuck did you get all that paper? And when was you gonna tell a bitch?"

André frowned. "You know I put a few stakes into the business account every few days to clean my drug money. Why the fuck I gotta kept reporting that shit to you?"

"A few stacks as in how much?"

"Nine."

"Nine stacks?" Olivia wasn't sure what was going on. When did nine stacks equate to nine hundred thousand? Nine stacks was nine thousand every day all day in the hood.

"Yo, you buggin' right now."

Olivia fumbled in her purse for the bank receipt and handed it to André. "When you say nine stacks, you mean almost a million dollars?"

André looked down at the receipt. "What the fuck is this?"

"You tell me."

"This ain't me!"

Olivia began to panic. "Then where did it come from?"

"Where did you get it?"

"It was on the receipt after I deposited the money from the shop. I thought you put it there."

"Where the fuck would I get a million dollars in cash? The tooth fairy?"

Olivia shrugged her shoulders. "I guess the bank made a mistake." Olivia sulked.

"When you say mistake, you mean that the printed balance on the receipt is the mistake, or the mistake is the actual funds are in our account?"

Olivia didn't know the difference. She hadn't thought that far ahead. "All I know is that it's wrong."

André's mind was racing. "Did you see if the funds were actually in our account?" he asked, his voice rushed and impatient.

"Well, I went to the teller and made a withdrawal and the receipt read the same as the first time. It read almost a million dollars."

"Did you ask her, were all those funds really in the account?"

"No, I just left to find you."

"Why the fuck didn't you handle your business before you come running over here?" he barked. "Why I always gotta be a fuckin' problem-solver? You got a nigga out here in this heat pondering over a piece of paper, when all your ass had to do while you were in the bank was find out if the money was there or muthafuckin' not! Now we're sitting here with this speculative shit! And for what reason?"

Onlookers began to stop and stare at the couple's heated argument.

"First off, muthafucka, you need to take it down!"

"Or else what?" André inched closer toward the petite Olivia.

"Don't push me, André!" Olivia put her hands on her hips, the independent woman's stance.

"Or else what?" André asked again. "Yo, just say the word, and you could be out. Just give me back the keys to your Maserati and leave with only what you came with."

"You know what?" She spun on her heels. "Fuck you!" she yelled, and stormed off.

"Olivia!" André screamed.

But Olivia never looked back.

André's mind was thinking a mile a minute. It was already past three o'clock on a Saturday. Banks were closed, so he had to wait out the weekend to find out what was up with all that dough being deposited into their account. He wanted to stomp a mudhole into Olivia's back. Instead, he let her walk away. For her always claiming how street-smart she was, she was looking like a real dumb ass to André.

Chapter 18

Monday morning couldn't come fast enough. Olivia and André walked into Chase Bank before making a small deposit.

This time Olivia spoke. "Could you give me my checking balance?"

The teller took out a piece of paper and wrote it down. When they read it, once again, over nine hundred thousand dollars—the couple was overjoyed.

Together they left Chase bank on 141st Street and began driving to midtown.

"What's the plan?" Olivia asked.

"Our plan is to get that money."

"But how?"

"What kind of stupid question is that?" André wanted his hands on that money so badly, he could smell it. "It's in our account, right?"

"But we didn't put it there."

He wanted to snap on Olivia but realized that he needed her to do all the transactions, so he adjusted his voice. "Look, I saw shit like this on television. You ever pay attention to those checks they send in the mail where they say you've won a million dollars and all you have to do is open up a subscription to a bunch of magazines and you could be entered to win money and prizes? But on the check they always print DO NOT CASH or VOID."

"No, not really."

André exhaled. "Anyway, I saw a *Dateline* episode or *20/20*, not really sure which one, but the company sent the check but didn't write

DO NOT CASH on the check. It was made out to a real person, and his smart ass went and deposited it into his bank account. The company's business account had the funds, and the money was transferred into the man's personal account. He then withdrew all that money, and there wasn't shit anyone could do to him because it was all legal."

"But we didn't get a check."

"But it's the same scenario. Somehow the bank fucked up and placed all that cash into our account. All we have to do is withdraw the funds before they realize it, and by that time, it'll be too late. And they can't do shit because we didn't steal that money. It ain't like we robbed a bank or nothing, so we can't get arrested."

"But what will the authorities say? Can't we get in trouble for knowing that it's not our money to take?"

"Not at all. Because it is our money. It has our name on it, and it's in our account."

Olivia thought about the logic. André was right. It was in their account and had their name on it.

"That money probably belongs to some rich muthafucka that has a similar account number as ours. He probably won't ever miss that money."

Olivia was getting amped. "What are we going to do with all that dough?"

"Let me worry about that."

At the midtown location, André told Olivia to go in the bank and ask for nine cashier's checks for one hundred thousand each, and the remaining fifty thousand in cash.

"With the fifty thousand, make sure you ask for large bills."

"OK, got it. Large bills." Olivia leaned in and kissed André. "Hopefully this won't take long."

André sat nervously inside Olivia's Maserati. They could have driven in his truck, but just in case they followed her outside, he wanted to look the part. And Maserati trumps Yukon all day.

One part of him knew that what Olivia was about to do was illegal as hell, but he told himself that he was only listed as a signer on the account. The account was opened in the business name, and Olivia was the sole account holder. In his line of work, he couldn't afford to get jammed up. He tried to tell himself that if the bank got wind of what happened, Olivia would only get a slap on the wrist but he, on the other hand, would face a severe penalty.

"I need to speak with the branch manager," Olivia said at customer service. "I'll be making a large withdrawal."

The attractive, well-groomed woman smiled politely. "Sure. Please have a seat."

Olivia sat down and steadied her breathing. If for any reason they told her that they'd made an error and the money wasn't hers to take, then no harm done. They still lived an opulent lifestyle.

Eventually a well-dressed white man in his early forties came out to speak with her. He extended his hand, and she shook it. "I understand you'd like to make a large withdrawal."

"Yes, sir, I would."

"Good. My name is Raymond, and you're?"

"Olivia. Olivia Robertson."

"Mrs. Robertson, would you come this way and follow me."

Olivia was led to a small corner office. Instinctively, she pulled out her bank card and license as Raymond logged on to his computer.

"How's your day going? Well?" Raymond asked, making small talk to the pretty young lady.

"Yes, it is. Thank you." Olivia searched for more words. "Have you been working at this bank long?"

Raymond paused in thought. "About eleven years."

"Wow! That's long. I've never committed to anything for that long."

"But you're married." Raymond focused on her ring.

"Yes. Newly married."

"I think you should work on that commitment thing," Raymond joked.

They both laughed at the light humor. Finally Raymond asked Olivia to input her security code, which she did. He remained expressionless as he examined her account, unlike the bank teller last week.

"So how much do you want to withdraw?"

"Nine hundred and fifty thousand."

Still no reaction.

"I'm assuming in a cashier's check?" Raymond fidgeted in his chair. He then asked, "Are you investing in real estate?"

Olivia didn't understand the question. "Excuse me?"

"Oh, I was just wondering if you were purchasing real estate. Especially in this market, I see a lot of our customers buying up real estate."

"No," Olivia replied. It wasn't any of his business what she wanted to do with *her* money. "And no to your first question. I want cash, not a cashier's check," she said, now feeling more confident.

"Cash?" Raymond's body language was that of concern. "We wouldn't be able to do almost a million dollars in cash today, Mrs. Robertson."

"Why do I have to wait for my money?" Olivia asked, her voice leveled and without any hint of hostility.

"Well, please understand we don't have that amount of cash in the vault. We could have the Dunbar armored truck make the delivery tomorrow morning. But I would still be concerned with you walking out of here with such a large amount of currency. Do you have security?"

"My husband and I could hire security. That's not a problem."

"That is solely up to you, but I would seriously consider it." Raymond stood up. "I'll make the request and have the funds here before noon. Would that work for you?"

"Yes, noon is fine."

"I'm assuming you want all large bills?"

Olivia smiled. "No way. I was thinking all in nickels," she joked.

"I'm just doing my job." Raymond smiled warmly. "We're taught to never make assumptions."

"I understand. I was just having a laugh at your expense."

"Certainly." Raymond once again smiled warmly. "Thank you for banking with Chase, Mrs. Robertson."

"My pleasure."

Olivia left the bank very proud of the professional way she handled herself. She realized that she had the ability to turn it off or on whenever she pleased.

As minutes turned into an hour, André thought about driving off. He couldn't understand what was taking her so long in the bank, yet he never saw five-O pull up.

Finally, Olivia emerged with a large grin on her face. Never had he been so happy to see anyone in his whole life.

"What took so long?"

"I had to wait for the branch manager."

"Where's the money?"

"I didn't get it."

"What? Why? Did they find out?"

"No, not at all. The money is still—"

"Well, did you put all of it in a cashier's check?"

Olivia rolled her eyes. "If you would let me finish my sentence, I'll tell you. I decided that I didn't want a cashier's check because then what?"

"Then what? Then we spend that muthafuckin' paper, that's what! What part of the plan didn't you understand?"

"Calm down. You always losing your cool for no freakin' reason. What I mean is, I want all cash. What's the point in withdrawing the money to put it in a check? To do what? Redeposit it into another traceable account?"

"So what happened?" André asked, sourly.

"He said to come back tomorrow."

"They gonna give you almost a million in crisp all-American dollars?"

"That's exactly what I'm saying."

"Yo, they do shit like that? People really walk out of banks with a million dollars in cash?"

"It's my money, isn't it? I can get it however I want it."

André laughed. "It ain't *your* money. It's *our* money."

Olivia no longer liked the way that sounded. And she didn't like André's earlier remark about him worrying about how the money would be spent.

While she was in the bank a few thoughts had rolled around in her mind, mainly, how dumb she was to even tell him about the money.

"How you figure? I mean, yeah, we're married, but the money was put into *my* account, and *I* found it. All you did was drive me here."

André wanted to choke the shit out of Olivia. He couldn't believe his ears. He backslapped Olivia's head into the window. "Say some stupid shit like that again!" André wanted to do more than slap her. The power he felt was palpable. "I wish you would try to flex on a nigga, after I pulled your raggedy ass outta the gutter. You'd be a bum-ass, bitch, if it weren't for me, so you better recognize. You don't even got the money yet and you actin' brand-new!"

Olivia didn't say another word, but her mind was churning. Slowly she was becoming a battered woman. A slap here, punch there, was now becoming more frequent. What her mother had said, "Once a man hits you, he will always hit you," was turning out to be true. And the last thing she wanted to be was an abused wife.

That night Olivia had few words for André. She thought about all her options, mainly, getting up early and making her way to the bank without him. With almost a million dollars at stake, who needed a drug-dealing husband with a "hand problem"?

Chapter 19

L as Vegas police and FBI agents were all convened at the local precinct, all working twelve-hour shifts, trying to solve the biggest heist of the century. The media attention alone had law enforcement almost desperate to nail someone—anyone—for the crime. The city's top brass wasn't about to let this case go unsolved. The tip hotline was receiving a flurry of calls, as the reward for information leading to an arrest had been increased from ten to fifty thousand dollars. If you were a criminal, you were being hauled in for interrogation. Law enforcement's behavior bordered on violating the civil rights of civilians, but they didn't care. It was all about closing the case.

They had successfully closed the Harrah's Casino attempted heist and were working diligently on solving the Bellagio heist. Other crimes, like the torching of the Super 8 Motel and murder, were put on the back burner. With every passing day, everyone was taking heat as the crime remained unsolved.

Libryis, Bellagio's insurance company, had hired several high-priced private investigators to gather any leads on their forty-six million dollars, annoying not only LVPD but the feds too. They didn't need yet a third unit with their hand in the cookie jar.

"We got a hit," Agent Peterson said as he walked into ground zero. "We ran a check on all the Bellagio's employees and came up with a paper trail on a Rosario Ortiz."

Detective Hernandez stopped in his tracks. "The fat chick?" He almost couldn't believe it.

"She works in housekeeping in the Bellagio. Why you know her?"

"She's one of the witnesses we interviewed just hours after the crime."

Peterson cut his eye toward Hernandez. "And you didn't pick up that she was hiding something?"

Hernandez ignored the sarcasm. He was in utter shock. Sure, Rosie had annoyed him, but he didn't sense she was hiding anything. "Honestly, I thought she was clean," Hernandez said. "What did you dig up?"

"We found nearly a million dollars transferred into her account just days after the heist, so unless she got a rich aunty who passed away, she's our number one suspect."

"Well, I'll go and pick her ass back up!" Hernandez didn't like being played.

"Slow your roll, rookie. Obviously this heist is for the big boys," Peterson said. The heist was a big jigsaw puzzle. They had to start from the end and work their way back to the beginning. "We already sent a car to her residence to pick her up. But do me a favor and pull her file. I want to read what she had to say, before I interrogate her."

"I want to be in on the interrogation too," Hernandez said.

Peterson shook his head. "Look, we got this. This is our lead, and we'll follow it through."

Now Hernandez lost his cool. His eyes were like slot machines they were moving so fast. "I don't need your fucking permission! I'll speak with my captain and make sure I can sit in. She's *our* witness."

"And when you had her, you didn't do shit!"

Agent Peterson had a slim body frame, but it was all muscle. He'd spent five years in the Marines before applying for the Bureau, and was proficient in karate and kick boxing.

Hernandez, on the other hand, looked intimidating. Just under six feet, he had broad shoulders and could bench-press three hundred pounds easily.

Before they could get into a full-on brawl, their colleagues intervened.

"Knock it off!" the captain stated. "We're supposed to be working in conjunction to solve this crime. The major is on our asses, and you two are acting like two pussies. When this crime is solved, neither one of you will get the credit. The mayor of Las Vegas will be up on that podium smiling and grinning for the camera and taking all the glory. Our instructions are to share intelligence and work together, so fuckin' share evidence and work together!"

Sergeant Aponte shared his information at the ready. "Well, when we interviewed her, she said that she was sure that the gang had stayed at the hotel probably weeks before the heist because the ringleader seemed familiar to her. She said she couldn't put her finger on it, but she was sure that he was a white male. With that little information, we got a subpoena from the judge and requested a copy of the name of every guest that stayed there in the past thirty days. Hernandez and I have been going over that list for the past couple weeks. We've been running each name and checking to see who has a criminal record."

"Well, clearly that's all bullshit." Peterson didn't want to buckle, despite what the captain had said. He felt that the Bureau outranked the PD in so many ways, it was almost insulting to let them share in his leads.

"Well, what about the other witness? Jasmine. Didn't you interview her?" Hernandez asked.

"Yeah. So?"

"So what about the Mexican theory? That could all be bullshit too. What if they purposely injected themselves into the investigation as a witness to throw us off?"

"Let's uncover one rock at a time. Right now we *know* Rosie is involved. Once we speak to her, we can bring Jasmine back in."

Peterson was dead set on the Mexican gang premise, and with Rosie being Hispanic, he wasn't going to let Hernandez dilute that theory.

♥♥♥

An hour later, two agents came back empty-handed.

"She's gone. Looks like she left in a hurry, like a thief in the night. We spoke to neighbors, and they said they haven't seen her in days."

Hernandez asked what everyone thought was a dumb question. "Are you sure she's gone?"

"She had a cat and apparently took it with her. We also stopped by the Bellagio, and she hasn't called in for work."

"When the fuck was the Bellagio going to let us know that?" Peterson said.

"Housekeeping just didn't think it was relevant to the crime."

"A bunch of morons!" Peterson hated being one step behind. He was still, somehow, blaming Hernandez. He felt that, had he interviewed Rosie, he would have picked up on her involvement. "I might know where she's gone. There was another account with a large deposit, someone named Olivia Robertson in New York. Could be family or a co-conspirator. Agent Scott, get on the phone with NYPD to meet us. We're on our way to New York."

"I'm going too," Hernandez said. "And I'm not asking your permission!"

Chapter 20

Olivia and André tossed and turned all night, both unaware of what the other was thinking. Olivia wondered if she got up early enough and snuck out to the bank without André, would he follow her there and make a scene. Perhaps tell the branch manager that the money wasn't hers. She figured that she wouldn't pack any of her clothing. All she'd do is snatch up all her diamonds, her designer pocketbooks, and peel out in her new Maserati. But even if André didn't follow her to the bank, what if she got there and was told that the funds were no longer in her account? That the bank had found its rightful owner? André would never accept her back. Not after knowing she'd tried to cut him out of the million dollars.

Olivia had so much on her mind. She needed to make the right decision, and soon. The clock read 4:03 a.m.

By 5:00 a.m., André was up and dressed sitting in the living room watching CNN. He no longer trusted his new wife. He knew that secretly she'd always held a grudge against him for marrying Honey, something she'd never forget, although she said she'd forgiven him. Her remark about keeping all the money for herself had thrown him, especially since it was free. She ain't work a day in her life for the money, yet she wanted to do him dirty. The more he thought about her words, the more infuriated he got. He wanted to wake her up and beat her senseless, but he needed her. There wasn't any way she could walk into the bank battered and bruised. No, he'd wait until he got his hands on the money, and from there he would treat her like the average bitch on the street.

André just couldn't shake the hate he was feeling. He'd been risking his life every day all day for that paper and then came and spoiled Olivia. And she just proved that she wouldn't do the same for him. He hated to go there, but Honey would have never done him dirty over no paper. Honey loved him unconditionally, and he was too immature to appreciate her.

♥♥♥

Finally, just past seven in the morning, Olivia walked into the living room to face André.

"Wonder what got you up so early?" she asked in a sour tone.

"Keep it up, Olivia, and I will stomp a mudhole in your ass, ya feel me? Keep talkin' reckless."

"Ain't nobody talking—"

"Shut the fuck up!" André roared. "I don't want to hear your annoying fuckin' voice for the rest of the morning. And fix a nigga some breakfast!"

André was more than ready to put the smack down. If Olivia kept giving him attitude, he was sure she'd live to regret it.

André didn't allow Olivia out of his sight until it was time for them both to leave for the bank. He'd shut off his cell phone because he didn't want any disturbances. In his mind there wasn't anything more important than the business at hand.

Olivia and André decided to forgo hiring security because if no one knew about the money then they felt they couldn't be at risk. And André knew better than to put his goons down with what was going on. He knew he'd end up with two bullets in the back of his head shortly after the withdrawal. No, the fewer the people knew about the money, the better.

On the way to the bank, all Olivia thought about was the pink cotton-candy-colored custom Range Rover with the snow-white buttery leather seats she would order first thing tomorrow from the dealer. She wanted to hear the engine purr like a cat while stunting on 125th. Olivia was filled with all kinds of joy, just salivating at her thoughts. She figured herself the black Barbie of the hood, and the pink Range Rover would paint the perfect picture.

To both their amazement, pulling out all that money went off without complication. Raymond asked that André pull their vehicle around to a private side entrance, and once Olivia signed all the necessary withdrawal information, several bank employees, along with the bank's security guard, loaded up the back of André's truck with nearly one million dollars.

André couldn't explain the exhilaration he felt. "It's on now!" he exclaimed once he got behind the wheel. Slowly he peeled out, heading north back to Harlem.

"My heart is beating like crazy!" Olivia placed her hand over her chest for dramatic effect. "I can't believe that shit was that easy."

André didn't comment. He was too busy in his own thoughts. He was going to invest about two hundred thousand back into cocaine, flip that, and make a profit. Stash about six hundred grand for rainy days, and with the rest, get some new bling. He'd spend at least a hundred grand at the Diamond District, buy some new gear, and go on vacation.

"You heard what I said?" Olivia asked.

"Nah, I ain't hear you."

"I said I want to go to the Land Rover dealer to order me a custom Range Rover in pink." Olivia clapped her hands together and began to giggle like a schoolchild.

André wasn't really feeling her after last night, and having the money in his possession, his disgust toward her had increased tenfold. He nodded his head like he was in agreement, but he wasn't.

When they pulled up in front of their house, André kept the engine idle.

"What? You not coming in?"

"Nah, I'm gonna go and put this paper up."

"Up where?" Olivia's eyes popped open in utter shock. "You not leaving with all this paper by yourself!"

"Yo, who the fuck you think you talkin' to? I ain't one of your little girlfriends! You keep pushing a nigga buttons and see what the fuck I do to you."

"Ain't nobody pushing your buttons." Olivia brought her tone down a notch. "But where are you taking all this money? Why can't you bring it upstairs to the safe?"

"You sound stupid," André replied. "That safe ain't built to hold this kind of paper. Besides, with this type of money, we'd be sitting ducks for all the stickup kids."

Olivia knew he was trying to play her. Since when a safe ain't built to hold money? All the kilos of cocaine he stored in that safe and revolving stacks of paper throughout the week. Not to mention, no one knew where they lived, so how would they get stuck up? But she didn't say anything slick to upset him.

"But you at least gonna let me know where you're putting all of it and also give me complete access, right?"

"Oh, no doubt. I'm storing it in my mother's basement. There's a large safe in there that's empty, with the same security code as the safe upstairs. So whenever you need anything, just go there."

Olivia thought for a second. She did have complete access to his mother's crib, but she wasn't sure she could trust his words.

"So why can't I go with you over there to unload it? You're gonna need help with all these bags."

"Nah, from there I gotta bounce to the Bronx to meet Hector and pick up some work. You know I don't want you around all that. Here." André got out the driver's seat and slid into the back. He opened up one of the bags and pulled out a few stacks, at least twenty grand, and handed it to her. "Go shopping or something and pick you up a few nice things."

Olivia smiled. "Thanks!" As soon as the words fell out, she wondered briefly, *Why am I thanking him?*

♥♥♥

André left, but he wasn't headed to his mom's crib. He was headed straight to South Orange, New Jersey, where Anita, his baby momma, lived.

No one knew about Anita, nor that he had a one-year-old son. He didn't even allow Anita to put his name on the birth certificate. The only telephone number she had on him was under a distant cousin's account, which he kept off at all times and hidden in a small stash box in his custom Yukon jeep.

André really didn't have any intentions of making Anita his girl. She wasn't his type. He was in Brooklyn fucking around with this shorty when he drove on to Kings Highway to get a hand detail-wash on his truck. On his way there, he saw a sign HAND CAR WASH held up by a crew of hot chicks all dressed in skimpy outfits and couldn't resist. He drove into the low-budget car wash instead of going to Kings Highway and began flirting with the young girls.

Watching them lather up his truck in their daisy dukes was turning him on, with their white T-shirts soaking wet and sudsy bubbles falling off their curves. It was all good, until they all pushed up too hard. All except one. She was intent on doing her job and not dressed half as provocatively as her peers.

Intrigued, he approached the shorty and found out that they all were foster kids, and their foster father owned the business. She was soft-spoken and hardly made eye contact with him. She didn't know her biological family and had been shuffled around all her life. Now she aspired to become a nurse.

André began taking out the plain Jane and, right before he got bored with her, found out she was a virgin. He had to have her. The first time they fucked, it was like pulling teeth, she was so tense. But her tight, wet pussy was addictive.

André began picking her up on the regular and soon found himself wanting to spoil her. But she was different. She wasn't materialistic like Honey or Olivia or the other broads he dated. She could care less about a Christian Louboutin or Gucci boots. She was into her books and wanted to make something of herself.

When André found out she was pregnant, he took her out of her foster parent's home and bought her a modest house in Jersey, far away from everyone. Anita cooked like she was Betty Crooker, kept a clean house, and took great care of their son. But what he loved most about her was, she gave him his freedom, never questioning where he was, or who he was spending his time with. He told her that he was in sales and had to travel, and apparently she believed that. He paid all the bills, her nursing tuition, and all their son's expenses, which was more than anyone had ever done for her in her life. For that, she remained loyal.

♥♥♥

It was still early when André pulled into their two-car garage. The tree-lined block with white siding homes and PVC fences was quaint. Anita was no doubt in school, and their son was at the babysitter. André took his time unloading his truck and loading up his safe in the basement. He had a room that was kept locked and which had a water- and fireproof safe, a room he called his "man cave."

When he was done, he fixed a sandwich, peered throughout the house, left a few thousand on the dresser, and peeled back out. He couldn't stay, knowing that if he was missing too long, on the heels of taking the money, then Olivia would become suspicious. He didn't know how he would handle Olivia, once she found out that the money wasn't at his mother's, but at the moment, he really didn't give a fuck.

Chapter 21

The twenty thousand dollars of free money was burning a hole in Olivia's pocket. No soon than André drove off, she jumped in her Maserati and called April.

"What are you doing?"

"I'm at work," April whispered. "Why?"

"You want to go shopping with me?"

April paused and then said, "Not really. All my credit cards are maxed out, and if I go, then I'll dig myself into more debt."

"What about Street? That nigga got paper. He should be taking care of you." Olivia already knew the 4-1-1 on Street. She knew he was no longer checking for April and was spending his dough on some new chick.

"I don't know what's up with him," April said honestly.

"What that mean?" Olivia said, pushing April to admit the obvious.

"He ain't returning my calls . . ." April's voice trailed off. Though embarrassed, she knew she had to face reality.

"Well, fuck him! Let's go shopping and buy some knew gear so that when he sees you, you're looking fly." Olivia said. "You know Chanel got its new line out, and it's to die for."

"Olivia, I can't. I just said I'm broke."

April was trying not to resent Olivia and her great life. She had a man who'd married her, which April and most others never thought would happen. And also André was a great catch. Half of Harlem was slinging their pussy his way, and yet he was taking very good care of Olivia.

"I'm trying to get my shit together. I've been working overtime, whenever they let me, to pay my bills, and then I'm going to start saving. Maybe open up my own business. I've been thinking about opening up a hair salon."

"A hair salon?" That didn't sit too well with Olivia. She didn't want anyone of her friends copying her moves. "But you don't know how to do hair."

"Neither do you."

"But at least I'm bilingual, so the Dominican women don't mind working for me!" Olivia couldn't hide her annoyance. "They'd never work for an all-black chick."

"Why don't you let me worry about that?" April no longer wanted to discuss her future with Olivia. "Look, Olivia, I'm at work. My supervisor is looking at me crazy. I have to go."

"Oh, OK, but real quick—If you come with me shopping, I'll pick you up from work and buy you a few things."

That piqued April's interest. Was cheapskate Olivia going to take her shopping? Why? "Seriously?"

"As VD."

"Olivia, thank you! I love you!" April couldn't contain her smile. "You know where I am. I get off at four."

The first stop in Bloomingdale's on 59th Street was the pocketbook section. Olivia spotted a red leather and crocodile Louis Vuitton bag with a four-thousand-dollar ticket.

"I have to have that," she exclaimed. "April, what do you think about this?" Olivia placed the bag over her shoulder and pranced around the saleswoman, smiling brightly. "Is this me or what?"

April studied the uniquely crafted bag and wished she could afford one. "You already know what's up," she replied. "See, this is why I gotta stay out these stores. Too much hot shit."

Olivia managed to purchase three high-end pocketbooks totaling eleven thousand dollars before heading upstairs to the Chanel section. April's eyes nearly popped out of her head when Olivia pulled out so much cash. Even the saleswoman was uncomfortable handling so much currency.

In the exclusive and quiet Chanel section, Olivia began pulling garments for herself as April just watched. She took a seat and watched as Olivia modeled several outfits for her. April wondered when Olivia was going to tell her she could pick out something or some things.

Finally, when Olivia was about to approach the cash register, April said, "Oh, you ready to leave?"

"Well, I gotta pay for this first." Olivia gestured toward the saleswoman. "I can't just walk outta here, right?"

The saleswoman joined in on the fun. "No, that wouldn't be a good idea, not unless you want to get detained."

April looked at the two and wanted to slap both their faces. "Well, I was asking because you said you were taking me shopping. That's the only reason why I came."

Olivia stopped midway through counting out over nine thousand dollars for her purchase. "You see me up in here buying all this stuff and now you gonna say you want something, after we've been in here all this time?"

"Excuse me?"

Olivia rolled her eyes. "I only got"—She counted out her last hundred dollars—"a little over a buck. And I know you can't get shit up here for that."

The saleswoman thought fast. If she could get that commission off the hundred dollars, why not? "Well, we do have some really cute headbands for just under a hundred dollars."

April couldn't believe her ears. "What do you mean, I didn't say anything? You asked me to come and said you were taking me shopping. You think I was standing here for my health?"

"I thought you were standing here as my friend. I didn't know I had to buy your friendship." Olivia tried to shove five twenties at April.

"Nah, that's all right. My bad." April's pride wouldn't allow her to take the measly hundred dollars. Besides, there wasn't much she could buy with it anyways. "I don't know why I even thought you were serious."

"What the fuck are you talking about?"

April shook her head. "You just sat in my face and spent almost twenty thousand dollars, and you're gonna try and play me and throw me a hundred?"

"Wait, hold up. This here my muthafuckin' money. I offered to do you a solid 'cause that nigga was doing you dirty. But you came up in here acting like I had to beg you to pick up something. You sat here watching me for hours and didn't say shit. Now you want me to feel guilty because I spent *my* money?"

"Olivia, please. You can try to turn this around like it's my fault, but we both know that you're a cheap bitch."

"And you're a broke bitch! A dumb-ass, broke bitch!"

"I'll take that." April nodded. "But anybody can be in my shoes—including you. You have it all right now, but don't get too comfortable, because what goes up must come down. You're the same chick who cried on my shoulders when André was dissing you. The same way he stepped out on his first wife is the same way he'll step out on you."

"At least I got a man."

"For now. My mother always said, 'The same way you get him is the same way you'll lose him.'"

"Really?" Olivia realized for the first time that April was jealous of her. "Really, bitch?"

"Really!" April began walking away. There wasn't any way she was riding in Olivia's car. "I got a train to catch."

Olivia couldn't be bothered with April's tantrum. She had a million reasons to be on cloud nine and knew that she'd get a whole host of haters once her and André began spending the money. She'd only spent a morsel of the money and look how April had reacted.

Chapter 22

Olivia thought that André would wake up in a bad mood as he did the day before, but to her surprise it was the complete opposite. She figured that as long as she didn't question him about the money, he would be nice to her. And although she wasn't going to ask about the money, that didn't mean she would forget about it. Olivia had every intention of sneaking over to his mother's house and taking half of the dough, perhaps more than half, and stash it in her own spot, far away from André. She didn't care if she got a beatdown. That type of money was worth a black eye any day. She just needed to do it at the right time, when she knew he'd be handling business for hours. Right now he seemed to not want to let her out of his sight.

"Yo, what you got to do today?" he asked.

"Nothing. I mean, I'm going into the shop as I always do. Why?"

"I wanted to go down to the Diamond District and snatch us up a few pieces."

Olivia couldn't resist. "How much you bringing?"

"About a hundred grand. Is that good enough for you?"

His sarcasm didn't get past Olivia. *If he could dish it out, then he should be able to take it.* "Is that all you, or is that hundred grand all me? I'm just askin'."

"There you go with that slick mouth of yours. What do you mean, all me or you? What kinda shit is you on?"

"I'm just asking where the money is coming from. I don't want to be thanking you for jewelry that I really bought. So are we going to the district with your paper, or you know, the paper that I got us."

André realized that Olivia was the type of chick his mother had always warned him about. The kind he could spoil for years with his drug money, and the moment he got jammed up, she'd leave him to rot in jail while she's fucking his best friend.

He loved that she thought she could outsmart him. He knew she was thinking every minute about getting her hands back on that money.

"Nah, this all me," he lied. "I told you I put that money up at my mom's crib for us. So either you coming or not."

"OK, I'm coming. Just give me thirty minutes to get dressed."

André could tell that Olivia tried not to show her excitement.

While Olivia was showering, he ran to his safe and emptied it into three black Prada duffel bags. He packed six keys of cocaine, all his jewelry, and eighty-five thousand dollars in cash. That took all of five minutes. Next, he grabbed all her jewels too. Anything of value that he'd purchased for her throughout the years—mink coats, Rolex watches, diamond tennis bracelets, everything. He then ran that down to his trunk before realizing that he didn't want to drive down to midtown with all that cocaine. He grabbed the duffel bag with the key's and ran that back upstairs just before Olivia emerged from the shower. After the Diamond District, he was out. He'd come back for the coke after he dropped her to her hair salon.

At first he was going to splurge on her with the bank money this morning, but once again, she put her greedy foot in her mouth. Now, he'd drive to the Diamond District, but he knew he wasn't going to buy shit. He couldn't wait to see the frustrated look on her face once she realized she was walking away with nothing.

André decided he was going back to New Jersey to live with Anita and his son and to chill from the drug business for a while. Just lay low until he needed to resurface. He knew there wasn't shit Olivia could do about his disappearance. He was a grown-ass man and could bounce if he wanted to. He'd leave Olivia to fend for herself and get a taste of her own medicine. Let her see how it felt to pay the mortgage or the note on her Maserati. Once she realized all he'd done for her, she'd be one sorry bitch. And there wasn't any way she'd go to the cops. What could she say? That her husband took her million dollars that wasn't hers? She'd implicate herself in a crime, and they wouldn't believe her anyway.

"Yo, hurry up! You got five minutes, or I'm leaving!"

"Wait! Let me just put on my earrings—"

"Nah, you don't need any of that. We're going to buy all of that, so why are you going to put on jewels. Damn!"

"OK, well—"

"Bye! I'm out."

Olivia came bolting right behind him, her hair still wet, her clothes not fastened properly, and her shoes in her hand. Inside André was laughing his ass off.

The warm summer afternoon with the sunny skies put André in the zone. He was bumping Trey Songz's last CD. He liked the song, "Can't Be Friends." He thought about all the women still mad with him for marrying Olivia. He was ready for his second divorce. He was a street dude. Who was he fooling? Next time around there'd be no next time. There wasn't any way he was taking another wife. Once you got hitched, women thought they owned you. He realized that he liked his freedom, the kind that Anita afforded him. *Why can't more women be like her?*

"You stopping at Jacob's or Manny's?"

"Nah, let's go and see Tito first," André stated. "I heard he got some new shit in."

André parked his Yukon in the No PARKING ZONE.

"You parking right here?"

"I just parked right here, didn't I?"

André jumped out, and Olivia followed, both thinking hateful thoughts.

"Police! Police! Don't fuckin' move! Put your fuckin' hands up! Both of you!"

In a nanosecond both André and Olivia were surrounded by NYPD—at least eight police cars—the FBI, and SWAT. A lot of things went through André's mind, some good, most bad. But his main thought centered on the 9mm Glock tucked in his waist. If nothing else, he was about to catch a gun charge.

Chapter 23

"Do you know why you've been arrested?"

"No," Olivia replied, her body shaking uncontrollably.

"But you never asked."

"Excuse me?"

Agent Peterson said, "We slapped the cuffs on you and your husband, haul you down to the precinct, have you sitting in a dirty interrogation room for hours, yet you never ask why you've been arrested."

"Because I know I didn't do shit."

"And that means what?"

"It means, I ain't do shit!"

"Or it could mean the opposite. It could very well mean you did a lot of shit, but you're not sure which shit you're being busted for."

"Look, I'm a businesswoman who owns my own hair salon, Olivia's, off 145th. You can check it out."

"Cut the crap!" Peterson bellowed. "Tell me about the heist!"

"The heist?" *Is that what they're calling it?*

"You better start talking, or I promise you, I'll make sure you do life!"

"How am I gonna talk about something I don't know about? I promise you, sir, I don't know about no heist." Olivia was less combative. She kept willing herself not to panic. André had tried to convince her that what they'd done was harmless, but deep down inside she knew better. No one takes losing a million dollars lightly but to have a dozen police officers, SWAT, and the FBI pulling guns on you seemed a little extreme. She thought that what they did was white-collar crime.

Weren't they supposed to be treated differently, with more respect?

Agent Peterson tossed a few glossy 8 x 10 photographs at her.

Olivia looked down and saw nothing but dead bodies. Could André have killed these people? She truly was at a loss for words.

"Don't get quiet now," Sergeant Aponte said. "You see those men? They all had families, and now they don't."

"I told you I don't know anything about this!" Olivia screamed, suddenly frustrated.

Agent Peterson inched his chair toward her and leaned in, finger pointed in her face. "Where the fuck did you get a million dollars? Huh, bitch?"

Olivia's stomach did a flip-flop. The FBI agent was intense. She honestly didn't know about any murders . . . well, at least not *those* murders.

The money, on the other hand, was a completely different story. Olivia figured that taking the money was small stuff compared to murder. And since she didn't kill anyone nor knew about the murders in question, then her only crime was spending some free money that was deposited into her account. White people did that shit every day. And, actually, it wasn't even that serious because she didn't put the money in her account. She wasn't the mastermind.

Olivia figured that she would've been in more trouble had she got caught boosting in Bloomingdale's. They didn't have shit on her.

"I want a lawyer."

Sergeant Aponte piped up. "This is your last chance to give us your side of the story. Are you sure you don't want to talk to us?"

"I said I want a lawyer. I ain't got shit to say. *Comprende?*"

Aponte gave it one last shot. His voice was bordering on whining. "OK, if you want it that way, but we're gonna have to book you with conspiracy—"

"Charge me with whatever you want! I want a lawyer!" Olivia put her hands over her ears, a childish gesture, and began humming, ticking everybody off.

"You know what?" Peterson's voice rose in aggravation. "You better start talking, or that's it. I'm charging you with five counts of felony murder, nineteen counts of attempted murder, armed robbery, conspiracy, wire transfer fraud, bank fraud, and whatever else I can think of!"

"I told you, I don't know nothin' bout none of the shit you talkin'!"

André was frustrated. This was way over his head. He did drug deals, sold that pure Colombian uncut cocaine to his associates and made a profit. Simple shit. Shit that niggas growing up in the hood learned at an early age. The shit Agent Scott was talking about, conspiracies and masterminding crimes, takes years to pull off and was over his head. He truly had a headache.

The tap on the door stopped the line of questioning. A uniformed cop walked in and whispered something into the detective's ear. André, never the optimist, wanted nothing but good news. He hoped that he was there to tell the detective that they'd caught the wrong people.

"We just intercepted a FedEx package addressed from Rosario Ortiz to you. In that package it has a few personal items—baseball cap, T-shirt, jeans—and in the jeans pocket is a Bellagio memo pad. Are you telling me that if we do a DNA sample on the men's clothing we found, it won't match you?"

"Hell muthafuckin' no, it won't match my ass, cuz I wasn't there! I don't know who this bitch is! I'm married!"

"What does that mean? You're married? Come on, a handsome guy like yourself don't cheat? You've never cheated on your wife?" Agent Scott asked. "And think about your answer because, if you want me to believe a word you say, then you can't lie about stupid shit."

André thought for a second. "Yeah, I cheat on my wife, but I ain't fuck no Rosario broad from Vegas! I don't even know how she look!"

"So somebody is setting you up?"

"That's exactly what I'm saying."

"Who do you think would do something like that?"

André shook his head. He was confused. "I don't know."

"And where did you get the money again?"

"I told you my wife handle all the money."

"So your wife could be setting you up?"

"Nah, she love a nigga."

"But I thought you said you were innocent and being set up."

"I am!"

"Then go over in your head the list of suspects. Where did you get the money? We found well over a hundred thousand dollars in your car, among other incriminating evidence."

André weighed his options. Even though they'd caught him riding dirty with that gun, he felt he could fight that with a good lawyer. And even if he had to cop out, he'd do a one to three, easy. But if they tried to tie him into that money, money they're saying came from some heist out in Vegas with dead bodies, with his record, they'd bury him. He'd be finished. He could rot in jail for years just fighting this case. And who the fuck was this Rosario chick? The only Spanish chick he knew was his wife and her family.

What if Olivia was setting him up to get knocked? She was the one who came to him with the one-million-dollars-just-appeared-in-my-account story. Could Olivia be working with the feds? He'd heard about shit like that. Right now he didn't know what to think, other than Olivia was behind all this bullshit and he played right into her hands. And how the fuck could a FedEx from some unknown broad with evidence be sent to him?

"Then Olivia set me up. All I know is, she said she had almost a million dollars in her account."

"Did you ask her where did she get a million dollars?"

"Hell yeah, I did. She said that her beauty shop been doing good."

"You want us to believe that she told you that she made a million dollars from doing hair?" Detective Hernandez asked. "And you believed her?"

"I ain't say I believed shit. You asked me what she told me. Of course, a nigga pressed her, and she kept to her story. Y'all in there interrogating her. I bet she ain't said shit! She sticking to her story. Either that, or she throwing a nigga under the bus."

"So where is the money? All of it?" Detective Hernandez asked.

"Ask Olivia. She runnin' things right now. She's gone on shopping sprees buying all types of expensive goods. Today was all her. She wanted to buy herself some more bling. Ask what a nigga bought outta the deal? Jack shit, that's what!"

Agent Scott thought for a second. "You know we'll check out your story, right?"

"That's what I want y'all to do. Investigate this muthafucka! My name ain't on shit. Olivia came to me on the basketball court talking about this dough. Olivia walked into the bank and made the withdrawal. Y'all feds and shit. Investigate this bitch, and you'll have a bunch of witnesses to back me up. She's tryin' to set a nigga up."

"Why?"

"She know a nigga ain't faithful. Maybe she on some get-back type shit."

"Why?"

"She never got over that I got married to my first wife while her and I were fucking around. I never even told her about Honey. She had to hear about us in the streets."

"Honey like a nickname. Your honey, like slang?" Agent Scott asked.

"Nah. Her name is Honey. My ex-wife."

Hernandez's interest was piqued. "And where is she now? Your ex? This Honey."

"The hell if I know. We ain't on good terms."

Bingo! Detective Hernandez thought. The same name as one of his original suspects was inexplicable. And she works in the Bellagio, was having an affair with the armored car driver, and was married to André Robertson, who had a million dollars of the heist money in his new wife's account. He needed to dig up more information on Honey, but right now, he didn't want to get off his line of questioning.

"How long have you been divorced from Honey?"

"The divorce was final over a year ago."

"What's her maiden name?"

André frowned. "Why?"

"Because we asked that's why!" Detective Hernandez snapped.

"Be easy, damn. Her name is Honey Brown."

"André, we're going to take a break and go and get lunch. We'll bring you back something too," Hernandez said.

"Nah, I ain't hungry. You wanna help a nigga out, unclasp these cuffs and open up these doors."

Detective Hernandez and Agent Scott left the interrogation room, but Scott was baffled.

"Why did you end the interrogation? We almost had him. I think at any second he would have confessed."

"I need to speak with Sergeant Aponte. He just mentioned that he was married to someone named Honey."

"Yeah, I heard that. And?"

"Well, Sergeant Aponte and I interrogated one of the blackjack dealers from the Bellagio. I had to call her back in when the wife of one of the murdered armored guards came in and said that her husband was having an affair with Honey Brown, something Ms. Brown failed to mention."

Agent Scott nodded his head. "This team is expanding day by day."

"Exactly. I'll have NYPD run all they can on her alias, Honey Robertson, and see what they come up with. Meanwhile, I'll fill Sergeant Aponte in on what we just found out. In the meantime we got what we needed on tape from André. I think we should pull Agent Peterson and Sergeant Aponte and send in two NYPD female detectives to interrogate his wife and let her listen to him sell her out. Once she hears about his cheating and also pointing the finger at her, I'm sure she'll roll on him in a heartbeat."

Chapter 24

As Detective Hernandez, Sergeant Aponte, Agent Peterson, and Agent Scott all convened in a small conference room so Hernandez could share the new intel he received, NYPD detectives Elise Fields and Alison Newton walked into the interrogation room where Olivia was seated.

"I don't know why they sent you two in here!" Olivia was antsy and aggravated from sitting on a hard chair for hours. "I told them I want a lawyer."

Speaking softly, Detective Fields began. "OK, we know what you want, and you know your rights. But did you know that your husband has rolled over on you, and we're about to charge you with conspiracy, five counts of felony murder—"

"What the fuck you talkin' 'bout, my husband rolled over? You expect me to believe that shit?" Olivia let out a mocking laugh. Her husband was a street dude. They didn't snitch.

Both detectives took a seat.

"Olivia, we wanna play something for you, and when we're done, if you tell us to fuck off, then we're out of here and you'll get your lawyer." Detective Newton pressed play on the tiny device. André's voice came booming through loud and clear, his words crisp and sharp, cutting Olivia like a knife. She couldn't believe how easy it was for him to snitch. She'd given him over a decade of her life. All the ups and downs she went through with him, and he spoke about her like she was some side chick. April's words began resonating in her head. André didn't give a fuck about her. He was a disrespectful womanizer. She should have known better than to fall in love with a man who took his mistress to fuck on the bed he shared with his wife.

Olivia began singing like a bird. She admitted that they had the money but denied knowing anything about the heist—which no one believed. But the main objective was getting their hands on as much heist money as possible and then handing off all the evidence to the assistant district attorney.

"He took the money to his mother's house yesterday. She lives at A-134 E. 133rd Street and Lenox."

Detectives Fields and Newton couldn't leave the room fast enough. They told that information to the detectives and agents on the case, who then went to the judge to get a subpoena to search his mother's residence, all the while André and Olivia sat.

Meanwhile, Detective Hernandez got Honey's background pulled and, to his surprise, found out she was a former ATF agent who was fired a few years ago, and married André Robertson seven years ago. They'd divorced shortly after he filed attempted murder charges on her, which were ultimately dropped. As everyone read through her file they found out that she was dished a raw deal. She was fired from the agency after leaving the field while on duty. She'd claimed that her supervisor tried to rape her, but her claims were unfounded and she was turned loose. From there she moved to Las Vegas and had kept her nose clean ever since.

"She's our mastermind," Detective Hernandez exclaimed. "I can feel it."

"Is that what you get after reading her file?" Agent Peterson asked.

"Isn't it obvious?"

"Actually, it's not. My read is that the ex-husband is the mastermind. Did you read his jacket? He's been in trouble since he was a juvenile.

Armed robberies, drug deals, and he's been questioned on a slew of murders. He fits the profile. Honey Brown's jacket is clean. She was a straight-A student, finished second in her class at the academy, and was on a good path until her run-in with her supervisor. And if you ask me, she didn't make that shit up about what happened in the field."

"She has the smarts to mastermind a crime on this level," Hernandez continued. "Robertson MO is drug deals not Vegas heists."

"Then why is the money trail leading to Rosario Ortiz, Olivia, and André Robertson? I bet if we dig deep enough, Rosario and Olivia have some sort of connection. Most likely from way back."

"Why? Because they're Hispanic?" Hernandez asked. "You're determined to pin this on a Latino. First the Mexican gang members, when one of the witnesses described white males!"

"Are you friggin' kidding me?" Peterson bellowed. "This isn't about race! Don't come in here playing that race card! I'm going where the evidence leads me, and it doesn't lead to Honey Brown!"

"And why not? Because she's one of yours?" Hernandez couldn't shake his intuition.

"You know, Hernandez, you're a moron. I don't know how you even made it to first-grade detective. You would have never made it at the Bureau."

When the plainclothes NYPD detectives came back from André mother's house, Detective Hernandez wasn't too pleased.

"We checked the house from top to bottom. It's clean. Olivia lied. The money isn't there."

"You still think your half-Latino princess is innocent? We got over forty million dollars out there, and this bitch think she can blow smoke up our asses and have us on a paper chase?" Peterson was done playing niceties. "She's going down!"

At that moment another set of plainclothes NYPD detectives came back with all the merchandise that Olivia had bought just the day before at Bloomingdale's along with the surveillance tapes on which Olivia is clearly seen counting out thousands of dollars and André isn't anywhere in sight.

As the detectives and agents looked at the tape, Agent Scott replied, "Find out who the friend is she's with. We'll want to get a statement from her." Then he added, "So far everything André Robertson is telling us about Olivia is adding up. She was the one who controlled and, up to date, was spending all the money."

"And the branch manager said she came in and did the withdrawal alone—"

"Although he did pick out her husband as waiting in the car."

"But he didn't sign for it. That's all her."

"OK, so who's the real mastermind here?" Sergeant Aponte asked. "It's either André Robertson, who has set up Rosario Ortiz and Olivia Robertson to take the fall for the measly million dollars each, while he rides off in the sunset with the remaining forty four million."

"Or it could be Olivia Robertson who never got over his infidelities and wanted to set not only André up but his ex-wife as well. Hit the casino she works at and allow the heat to surround her."

"Nah, that doesn't make any sense. Why would she deposit the money into her own account?"

"That's a good question. But why did she send us on a wild goose chase at his mother's house?"

"What about André? My money is on him. He's the real mastermind. He set up Rosario, Honey, and also Olivia to take the fall, while him and his crew gets away with murder and the money. And the cherry on top was murdering his ex-wife's new piece of dick, Brian. And depositing the money into Olivia's account would make Honey look like she was extracting revenge." Agent Scott had made up his mind.

Hernandez just couldn't fully swallow the theories. The level of sophistication was too advanced for a coke dealer. And where was the remaining heist money?

Just then another NYPD detective came in to share more good news. "We just found a safe at the Robertson residence. Our safe cracker got it opened and found six kilos of uncut cocaine inside."

Everyone smiled at that realization.

"He's going down!" the detective replied.

"Not so fast. Only Olivia Robertson's name is on the mortgage for that property. If he gets a good lawyer, the charge won't stick."

"Send in the latent print guys and see what fingerprints are pulled off the safe. My guess is that both their prints will be there."

"And he could argue that he only used it to store important paperwork and once again throw the weight on his wife. She'd need to testify against him, but you see she's playing games! We let her listen to him sell her out, and still she spits in our face and sends us on a wild goose chase for the million dollars."

"Maybe she's not as innocent as we think." Sergeant Aponte concluded.

"That's a possibility. OK, here's what we're gonna do. Have ballistics check his Glock to see if it has any bodies on it. It could have been used in the Bellagio heist. In the meantime, all we could really charge him with is the gun. Charge Mrs. Robertson with the Bellagio heist, conspiracy, felony murders, attempted murder, and the six kilos of cocaine. Once she sits in jail for a while, she'll start to roll over on everyone involved. And if Honey Brown is involved, she'll be able to prove that. We'll have her expedited to Vegas first to get arraigned there on a federal level due to the magnitude of the crime, and then she'll come back to New York to get arraigned on the drug charges and stand trial in the state court.

"Meanwhile, there's still a warrant out for the arrest of Rosario Ortiz. I'd love to have her captured so we could interrogate her the proper way," Peterson remarked dryly. "And once she's arrested and faced with the preponderance of evidence, if your suspect is involved, then Ms. Ortiz could give up that testimony as well. Also, we'll have our IT do a search and cross-reference everyone involved telephone records, including that of Ms. Brown."

Hernandez knew that was all they could do at the moment, but somehow he felt that they wouldn't come up with anything substantial on Ms. Brown. She was former ATF. He didn't think she'd be foolish enough to have telephone records, or anything else for that matter to connect her to this crime.

Agent Scott and Detective Hernandez walked into the interrogation room holding André.

"Stand up and place your hands behind your back."

"What am I being charged with?"

"For now, that loaded nine millimeter!"

André was actually relieved.

Agent Peterson and Sergeant Aponte walked into the interrogation room holding Olivia.

"Mrs. Robertson, stand up and place your hands behind your back. You're going to have your chance to speak with your lawyer."

"What?" Olivia began to panic. "Why? Why are you arresting me? I ain't done shit!"

"Tell it to the judge," Peterson said.

Epilogue

The news of Olivia and André's arrest had filtered back to Honey in Vegas. She was a little shocked that André wasn't charged with more than just a gun but equally shocked that Olivia was the only one taking the fall. She felt she'd given them more than enough evidence to jam them both up; but she knew that they wouldn't just let André walk for long. They'd stay on his ass until they exhausted all their options.

Honey was certain that once Olivia was convicted she'd work out a deal to testify against André and bring him down with her. She'll be so shocked that she's sitting in jail and he's not, Honey was sure that Olivia will think that André had set her up and want to turn state's evidence. So, either Olivia would handle André, or Honey would finish him off for good.

♠♥♣

In Vegas, Olivia and Rosie's pictures were splattered across every local paper. They were calling Olivia, "El Mastermind." Somehow the FBI had made a connection to a Spanish gang that had probably fled to South America with the heist money. Rosie was placed on the FBI's Ten Most Wanted list, and reported sightings of her were coming into the Bureau daily. The papers speculated on Olivia's husband, André, but reporting that police still considered him a suspect.

♠♥♣

Honey was able to begin setting up her life. She'd purchased a modest, three-bedroom beach house in the island of Antigua, overlooking white sand and baby blue skies. Meanwhile, back in the States, she began filtering small increments of money into Stephon's business. Two thousand dollars here and there to start leasing more luxury vehicles. He never asked where the money was coming from, but if he did, she had an honest answer. Blackjack. Honey wasn't so dumb as to invest any of her heist money into his business, because she was sure she was still under suspicion.

For now Honey divided her life between Antigua and Vegas. She was biding her time for when she could make a clean escape from Vegas and set up her new identity on the beautiful little island.

As agreed, Honey didn't hear from the other girls, and that was a good thing. She knew that everyone was doing well; they'd risked too much to throw it all away on foolish things.

Just as Luther had promised, he gave Chief an amazing funeral that Honey didn't attend, and from there he headed south and opened up a body repair shop and bought a modest house overlooking a lake. To Honey's surprise, Cinnamon and her daughter followed Luther south and were living together as husband and wife. Cinnamon was the type that needed guidance and structure, and Honey could understand how she gravitated toward her father. She also realized a young girl like Cinnamon with all that cash could have easily spelled disaster.

Honey walked out into the hot desert heat after she got off the night shift at the Bellagio. Detective Hernandez, who was parked parallel to her Camry, sat perched on the hood of his late-model Ford Mustang.

As she approached, he hopped down and leaned on his passenger's side door. "I'm watching you, Brown," he stated.

"Good. Then I know I'll always be safe."

"You think you're clever." He rubbed his chin. "But there is no such thing as a perfect crime."

Honey stopped in her tracks. "For the last time, I don't break the law. I used to enforce it."

Detective Hernandez laughed mockingly. "I ain't buying that bullshit you trying to sell. It's just a matter of time before I nail your ass to the wall. Just a matter of time before I come for you."

Honey shrugged. "And just hypothetically speaking"—She paused and glared into his eyes, so he could feel her words. "If or when you do come for me, do you seriously think I'll just let you take me?" Not allowing him to answer, she added, "Never forget my field training, Hernandez—because I don't. Please don't underestimate me."

Hernandez's laugh was full of sarcasm. "I'll come like a thief in the night."

"You'll have to come harder than that."

"Maybe I will," Hernandez said under his breath. "Maybe I will."

TEAM MELODRAMA

BAD APPLE: THE BADDEST CHICK
BY NISA SANTIAGO
OCTOBER 2011

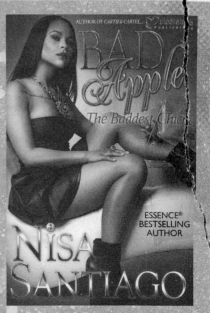

SHEISTY CHICKS
BY KIM K.
DECEMBER 2011

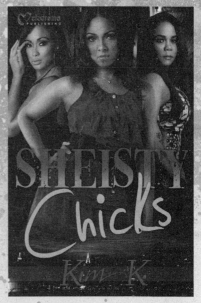

WIFEY: FROM MISTRESS TO WIFEY
BY ERICA HILTON
NOVEMBER 2011